# The Girl Who Swam to Atlantis

Elle Thornton

ISBN: 1-4664-3168-7
ISBN-13: 9781466431683

dedication: For Emmett Till
We Must Never Forget

# Contents

# Chapter 1
# Marine Base, North Carolina, 1957: Spies

The leaves are beginning to show red and yellow now, but in my heart it's still summer in North Carolina, and I've just seen Hawkins for the first time. He is standing beside the river. My new friend Trish and I watch him reach for a cigarette in a pocket of his Marine fatigues. He lights it and smokes, his gaze fixed on the water. We make faces and elbow each other behind thick bushes. Spying seems funny until he spins around on his long legs and strides toward our hiding place. He stops about six feet away.

"You in there, make yourselves known. And be quick about it." With the toe of his heavy combat boot, he grinds the cigarette to shreds in the sandy dirt.

Trish tugs at my T-shirt sleeve and gestures toward the woods behind us. She wants us to get out of here. But if I try to run, I believe he'd catch me for sure. Besides, I want to talk with him some because of the way he's been looking at the river, kind of like it has him under its spell. Well, that sure is true for me.

I pull away from Trish and stumble out of the bushes.

Below the brim of his military cap his face is in shadow. But I can see his fierce scowl and the jagged scar that rolls from one eyebrow to the corner of his mouth. It cuts deep into his brown skin. He sets his big hands on his hips and looks down at me. "Tell me who you are, young lady."

"I'm Gabriella." I make myself sound bold, but I've done an about-face on the topic of running. I'm seriously thinking it over right now. Then Trish steps out of the bushes. "And this is Trish."

"You can call me Hawkins." His voice is rough.

Trish taps the face of her wristwatch. "C'mon. I've got to go somewhere."

Hawkins nods. "All right, then, you two young ladies try and stay out of trouble." I think I see a slight smile, but he's turning away from us and I can't be sure.

Three swept-wing fighter jets shriek low overhead. Hawkins takes off his military cap and wipes sweat from his brow. He sets the cap back on his head as he watches the jets soar beyond the blue wall of sky. Then he walks to the river where it makes a pool beneath the limbs of leafy trees.

Trish is already trotting through the woods. When I catch up with her, we both start laughing about our encounter with the scar-faced man. We're puffed up with ourselves like the pale mushrooms growing from the forest floor.

Trish pops a stick of Juicy Fruit gum into her mouth. "Let's race."

Just then a gust of wind makes the trees creak. Long pieces of curly gray moss flutter from twisted branches like hairs torn from a head.

We yell and whirl away. Ahead of me Trish's sturdy legs pump like engines. I can't believe we're both going into seventh grade in the fall. She's big all over. She even wears a bra.

We bust out of the trees between a garage and a one-room building. There's a cardboard box on its doorstep. A path leads directly between the small building and the kitchen at the general's quarters. That's where I live.

Tall pines grow in the yard. We walk under them toward the front of the house, and I ask Trish about getting together again. She's going out west with her family. She'll call in a few weeks when she gets back, she says, and I watch her run home through the pines.

Upstairs in my room I drop onto a narrow bed. I nap until clattering from the kitchen below wakes me. I wonder who's down there. I know it isn't Mama cooking supper. And it isn't the general.

In the trenches of my brain I think of him as the general instead of father or dad. He wears silver stars on his uniform. He watches over hundreds of men, jets, and helicopters. His job is to make sure they're ready to fly and fight. Everyone salutes him.

When he's annoyed there's this muscle that sometimes snaps in one side of his jaw. Muscles in both sides of his jaw snap when he's extra annoyed. But he's never raised his voice in anger at Mama or me.

His voice reaches me now as I start toward the stairs. "Gabriella, get a move on. Chow time."

"Yes, sir."

At the bottom of the stairs he grasps my elbow and steers me to the dining room. We sit at opposite ends of a long table. The kitchen door swings open, and a tall man strides into the room carrying a silver pitcher.

As he fills our glasses with ice water, my face grows hot. It's the man I'd spied on and laughed at with Trish. After pouring water, he serves us meatloaf, potatoes, and green beans. I keep my gaze stuck to my plate like weeks-old gravy and grits. I don't like being waited on.

"Hawkins, have you stowed your gear yet?"

It's rare when the general speaks, so I look up from my plate.

"Yes, sir." Hawkins turns his head in the direction of the little building at the place where Trish and I came out of the woods. The cardboard box is no longer on its doorstep.

"Just say the word if you need anything."

"I'll do that, sir."

"By the way, this is Gabriella, my daughter. Gabriella, this is Hawkins."

"I met the young lady and her friend this afternoon."

The general frowns. "They didn't make a nuisance of themselves, did they?"

"No, sir."

Hawkins leans a shoulder into the kitchen door so that it swings open. He steps inside. The door swings closed, cutting off the sound of music from a radio and the whir and click of a metal fan.

The general pushes his plate to one side. There's still plenty of food on it. A lighted cigarette balances in an ashtray next to his plate. His face is gray and tired.

I tell him about Trish. He doesn't say anything until I stand and start to carry my dirty dishes toward the kitchen.

"Hold on. Just what do you think you're doing?"

"Trying to make myself useful, sir."

"You are to stay out of Hawkins's way. Let him do his job. And don't ask him to do anything special like make cookies, cakes, and pies for you and your friends. Do I make myself clear?"

I about roll on the floor snorting. Why would I ask Hawkins to make cakes and pies? I want the general to see *me* being helpful and doing things really well on my own.

"But, sir," is all he allows me to say.

"Gabriella, you are to sit down until you are excused." He waves in the direction of my chair.

If only I can show him I'm good at doing something on my own, I feel sure he won't send me north to St. Agatha's Boarding School for Girls again in the fall. Also, if I help out in the kitchen, no one can call me a spoiled general's daughter. And Mama always likes it when I fix meals for her and do the dishes.

At the far end of the table the general stares out the window into the growing darkness. Mama told me he sometimes goes far away in his thoughts to be with his men from the big war and Korea. Tendrils of smoke drift across his face from the cigarette that burns forgotten in its ashtray.

I set the stack of dishes on the table. And I sit down.

# Chapter 2
# The River Calls

I jump from the back porch steps to the lawn. The garage, Hawkins's quarters, and the woods where Trish and I raced are to my left. Straight ahead at the edge of the lawn a steep slope plunges below to a beach and the wide river.

I make my way down the slope, cross the beach, and wade in. The water's warm, the sandy mud soft on my feet. A branch of the river flows from the woods, and I follow it. Soon I find Hawkins in the same place Trish and I spied on him yesterday. He's sitting on a log with a fishing pole and bucket behind him on the ground. An open book rests on his knees.

I push through the bushes. He turns swiftly to look across his shoulder at me, and I stroll to his side.

"Hello, Miss Gabriella."

"How come you weren't in the kitchen earlier this morning?" I was relieved to fix breakfast for myself, but I'm curious as to why he wasn't there.

Hawkins places a marker in the book on his knees. He closes the book and sets it on top of a piece of paper on the ground. Then he turns around on the log so that he's facing me.

"The general allows me mornings off, young lady."

Yea! This means Hawkins won't be serving breakfast. But will he hog the kitchen the rest of each day? What he says next makes me believe he's read my mind.

"He's also giving me time to work other jobs for the extra pay when something comes along, like tending bar or serving at lunches and dinners."

I can't keep myself from grinning. What would he say if he knew I want him to go away, forever?

Hawkins finds a cigarette in a pocket of his fatigues. He bows his head to light it and takes a deep drag. Raising his head, he releases a thin stream of smoke.

He looks steadily at me. "Miss Gabriella, something tells me you're unhappy with my presence at your quarters."

I don't know how to tell him what's on my mind, how I want to show the general I'm good at things so that he won't send me away to boarding school again, how living in a big house and being waited on makes it seem like I'm spoiled, and how I want to cook for Mama when she gets home. I hug my arms to my chest and think these things over.

Hawkins seems like he's about to say something more. Whatever it is, I don't want to hear it.

"Well, I'm shoving off now," I tell him. And I hurry away, leaving Hawkins behind.

I wander along the river until I find a place that's shallow enough for me to see the bottom. I shed my shorts and pull off the shirt covering my bathing suit.

The suit's faded, stiff, and scratchy. I feel sure it's made of tent canvas left over from World War I.

I splash around in the water, and before long I'm thinking of the time Mama took me swimming at night in the ocean. I dog-paddled through the waves. But I couldn't keep up. I couldn't reach her.

My skin goes bumpy like a plucked chicken in the icebox, and I climb out of the river to sit on the beach and warm up in the sun. Two dragonflies hover and dart away. Overhead, fighter jets thunder across the sky. The jets vanish. Silence settles deep inside the woods.

Then the song of cicadas braids the long green shadows. Behind me there's the sound of bushes whipping against material. Twigs snap. I look to see who's there.

Uh-oh. Isn't there anyplace I can go without his showing up? He's invaded the kitchen, the dining room, and now my patch of the river.

"The fish are jumping right in this very spot, Miss Gabriella. I thought I'd try my luck."

I hadn't seen any fish, and I sure don't want to be near where he is. But the sun is warming me here. I decide to stick around to see if he actually catches anything.

"I'm going to bring a nice fish home for my lunch. Fresh caught and cooked in some butter with herbs and bread crumbs, it'll be real tasty."

This information has me clamping a hand over my mouth. I'm nearly gagging at the thought.

He's at the water's edge, glancing back at me. "My number three sister, Lily, doesn't care for fish either."

"Number three?"

"There are five girls in all."

Hawkins turns to cast his line out across the water. He's only a few feet from me. I can hear all that he says.

"Practically from the time she was born Lily was wild to swim. All the while she was growing into a young lady, we worried about her swimming alone. But if someone told Lily that swimming by herself might not be a good idea, she'd say, 'uh-huh' and do what she pleased." He glances across his shoulder and levels his eyes at me. "It could be you and my sister are somewhat alike."

"Well, maybe," I tell him. Then I explain that Mama's a great swimmer, and she has told me and the general I'm almost as good as she is. "She's said I only need to practice what she's showed me about swimming and being careful, and I'll be fine." As I tell Hawkins this, I'm thinking I sure would like to believe her, but I have doubts.

Hawkins is frowning. He sets the fishing pole aside and lights another cigarette. He smokes it while walking up and down the beach. The scar on his face appears red as flame. He looks at the water. He glances at me. After a while he nods, like he's made up his mind about something. He drops the half-smoked cigarette, buries it with the toe of his boot, and sits beside me.

"One day Lily asked me to show her how to improve her swimming. She didn't know it, but that day she helped me, Miss Gabriella."

"She did?"

"Showing her a few swim techniques made me proud." He looks up and down the river. "I gave her a few pointers in a place like this. It didn't take long before she was cutting through the water like a knife."

As he talks I'm thinking, *Hawkins could teach me like he taught Lily. When I've learned to swim really good, the general will be impressed with what I can do, and he'll let me stay at Rock Point for the school year. No more boarding school. I'll be here when Mama gets back.*

"So what sort of things did Lily let you show her?"

Hawkins gets to his feet. "All right, young lady, I'll be glad to demonstrate."

I listen carefully as he gives an overview of something called the American crawl. Then he goes through a series of moves, once, twice, and again. His long legs and arms make it easy for me to follow.

One thing he shows me is proper breathing. Watching his arms alternate in the same semicircle rotation, I see that as I draw one arm back and raise my elbow, I'm to slightly turn my head toward my shoulder and breathe in through my mouth. With that arm then moving forward and down and my other arm drawing back, I'm to exhale through my nose and mouth in the water.

Soon I'm ready to try what he's shown me. I wade in. But I cling to old habits. My hands paddle like I'm wearing mittens. My feet splash fountains of water. I climb out and drop down on the beach. "I can't seem to get the hang of it." I punch my fist into my palm.

Hawkins scowls. "Young lady, you haven't given yourself a chance. You need to get back in there and try again. Above all, eliminate 'can't' from your mind and your vocabulary right now."

"Yes, sir." I almost salute as I stand up.

"Hold your hands with the fingers and thumb like this." He lifts his hands and I think of dippers. "Keep your legs close together and move them up and down through the water. Remember, ankles should be flexible. And try for a small kick. No big splashes."

I start over. Kicking, bringing my arms forward and down and back and forward, reaching out, pulling, breathing the way he showed me. After awhile I'm sliding through the water.

It seems I'm in the water a long time before he stops calling instructions. Then I climb out and go to him at the river's edge.

I glance at him. The air is thick with humidity. His face and scar are wet with sweat. Something about the scar and the way the river moves with a slow whispering sound have me thinking of a story I'd heard just before school let out for the summer.

Our teacher told us about a young teen whose killers beat him and shot him before shoving his corpse into a river in Mississippi. The boy had whistled at a white woman, the teacher said. Our teacher told us the boy's name. I don't remember it now.

Hawkins is saying it's time for him to go. "You won't go in alone will you, Miss Gabriella." His eyes are hard as river rocks as he looks at me. He's not asking me a question.

"I promise. Will you show me more another day?"

"All right, young lady. All right, then."

Sometime in the night I wake from a dream of mermaids diving through waves. I remember wanting to follow, but the mermaids moved too fast for me. Then Hawkins calls me in from the shore. There's a boy with him. The boy's face is scarred. I swim to where Hawkins and the boy wait. But when I reach the shore, Hawkins and the boy are gone.

# Chapter 3
# To the Base Pool

*She's at the dining room table smoking a first cigarette of the day. Seeing me she'll say, "Darlin', let's you and me go find us a bunch of rainbows." She'll pour something from a bottle into a small glass, tilt her head, and drink it down. Mermaid hair curls around her face. The Japanese robe she wears shows blue waves rising along the sleeves. I'll fix us sandwiches.*

I haven't seen Mama since spring when the general sent me back to St. Agatha's. Ever since I can remember, she's gone away from time to time. I don't worry anymore that she might never come home. Mama won't stay away much longer this time. I just know it.

I push against the kitchen door making it swing open. Inside, a fan whirs and clicks on the counter. The general's left me a note taped to the icebox: "You are to use this money for lunch at the snack bar. Dad." Some coins are on the counter. I pocket them.

I've already stepped out the front door on my way to the club swimming pool when I find myself racing instead around the side of the house and between the tall pines. I'm heading to the slope at the edge of the lawn. The river flows wide below.

I make my way down the slope and run along the beach, then stop to wade in the tea-colored water. The sound of cicadas rises from the woods behind me. When Mama comes here she'll collect driftwood and stones for decorating. She'll make our quarters into a home. After a while I re-cross the hot sand of the river beach and start climbing to the lawn.

There's a man at the edge of the lawn gazing through binoculars slung around his neck. What does he see? I wave to him. When I reach the lawn, he's on the porch steps about to go inside at neighboring quarters. I guess he didn't see me. I walk to the club.

The smell of frying food and the steady thump of the diving board lead me to the snack bar, deck, and pool. They're at the bottom of a long flight of concrete steps. I walk down the steps and stop at the snack bar. From its shade I watch herds of kids splash in the pool. I see mostly little kids and their moms. Some older teens hurl a volleyball.

In the locker room I change into my swimsuit. Outside again in the sunlight I use the pool ladder at the shallow end and climb into the cold bright water. I hang onto the rim and practice kicking the way Hawkins showed me.

From behind me someone yells, "Watch out!" I turn in time to see a volleyball spinning my way. It lands within inches of my shoulder, making waves. A guy with short blond hair detaches himself from the group of older teens and swims over. When he reaches my side, he looks at me intently.

"Hey, you're okay aren't you?"

"No problem." I grab the ball and toss it to him.

Someone calls, "Doyle, you still playing?" Doyle sends the ball flying and the game heads to the deep end.

As he swims off to join the others, Doyle calls to me, "See you later."

I practice swimming in the shallows until dodging little kids grows tiresome. In the locker room I hurry out of my suit and into my clothes. There's a bulletin board beside the long flight of concrete steps. Earlier, I hadn't stopped to look at any postings. Now a notice with the words Swim Meet in bold letters attracts my attention. It's at the lower end of the bulletin board, and I lean down to see what it says about the event: Date And Time TBA. Look For Sign-Up Sheet.

From the corner of my eye I see a pair of wet feet below skinny legs approaching. The feet stop near me. I straighten. It's the guy I talked with from the volleyball game.

"You're new here," he says.

"Well, it's my third day."

"A veteran, then."

We exchange names.

"Gabriella Winter," Doyle says. "Have you been to the river?"

"I can hardly stay away."

"I go down there to practice guitar," Doyle says. "I'm learning from some of the stewards here."

Just then a steward walks over from the snack bar to ask Doyle if he could take a look at the jukebox. It's been acting up.

"Between us, Clarence, we can fix it." He looks over at me, "See you again, Gabriella?"

"Well, sure. At the river."

They haven't gone more than a few steps when I hear Clarence saying to Doyle, "Now what kind of invitation was that? We've got work to do on your manner with the ladies."

I take another look at the swim meet sign. I'm thinking I've got work to do too.

# Chapter 4
# Eula Mae

The general's telling me to get myself next door and "look after Eula Mae." Her son, Colonel Perkins, has an important meeting, and the nurse that cares for his elderly mother won't be in today.

"Yes, sir." I hang up the telephone and run next door.

From the shadowed screen porch I follow a hall to a dark bedroom. A small figure in a bed near a window huddles beneath some blankets. I'm not sure I'm looking at a live human until I step closer and find myself staring into a pair of large glittering eyes.

"Who are you, my dear?"

"Your neighbor Gabriella Winter come to look in on you. Are you okay, ma'am?"

"No, I am not. But if you will open that window and then make us tea, I shall immediately improve."

"Yes, ma'am."

I release a shade and shove the window up. A puff of air stirs the lace curtains in the window, and I hear something that sounds like the name "Jonas."

Eula Mae's face is motionless as the doll on a bookshelf in a corner of the room. I figure the sound is just the whispering wind. The wind moves on and she reaches a frail hand toward me.

"You'll find tea things near the stove."

In the kitchen a china teapot decorated with roses and a matching creamer, sugar holder, cups and saucers are on a tray. I boil water for tea and find cheese, mustard, and bread for sandwiches. Eula Mae definitely needs fattening up.

From a window above the sink I watch a boy and girl next door chase each other around a red Chevrolet parked in the driveway. They honk the car horn a couple of times. This doesn't go on for long before a man rushes out.

He yells, "Caitlin, B.J., get inside." The children punch each other on the arm as they race indoors. I carry the tray to Eula Mae's room and set our tea and sandwiches on a table beside her bed.

She struggles to sit up.

"Here, let me help you."

I place my arms beneath her arms and slide her upright. It's like holding a bunch of scarves close. She smells of lavender.

There's a straight-backed chair against a wall. I carry it over to the bed and sit while filling cups with tea. As if by magic a silver flask appears in Eula Mae's hand. She pours amber liquid from the flask into her cup. I add tea. She drops lumps of sugar in the mixture and drinks it down.

After a second helping from the flask, she blots her mouth with a napkin and settles against her pillows. The sandwich is uneaten. The flask disappears.

"My hearing's not sharp as it once was, but if you will speak and enunciate clearly, I would like to hear your life's events."

Even though I'd just gulped a steaming cup of tea and feel damp from being overheated, I immediately freeze up. The problem is I don't have any events to tell about. I step to the window and glance at the river for inspiration. At that moment its surface shines with light. I take a deep breath, as if I'm about to dive underwater. Something in me wants to tell about the river.

I return to my chair beside her bed and begin to describe where the river widens into a pool and how Trish and I spied on Hawkins there.

"Well, ma'am, he found us out. We were nervous because he looks fierce with a terrible scar on his face. Later on, you'll never guess who walks into the dining room from our kitchen."

Eula Mae's eyes sparkle. I suspect she knows the answer, but she lets me have the fun of telling her. "Who was it?"

"The man from the river. He's a steward at our quarters, ma'am. And he's showing me how to swim better. His name's Hawkins."

I tell her about my need to prove to the general I could do something well, how it might persuade him to let me stay at Rock Point with him and Mama. He'd see I didn't need any more fancy schooling far away because I know what it takes to be excellent at something.

"I just know Mama will come to Rock Point soon."

Eula Mae shifts her gaze to the river, and I'm not at all sure how much of what I'd said she's actually heard. But then her eyes meet mine, and she says, "I hear in your voice how much you love your mother." She'd even heard what I hadn't said out loud in words.

I had never thought of such a possibility as being able to *hear* love. Well, it makes me sit up straighter to have learned this. But the truth is my heart isn't always full of love for Mama.

"From what you've told me, Hawkins wants to help you. I had such a friend, too, when we both were children at Brightfields. He and I..."

Eula Mae looks toward the door and breaks off before she's told her story. The man standing just inside the room is small-bodied with round eyes that seem to bulge from his long, narrow face. His skin gives off the smooth whiteness of a sheet. I hadn't heard his footsteps.

"Hello, Mother." It's the colonel, her son, and I'd seen him once before when he was at the edge of the slope looking through his binoculars. He crosses the room to the foot of Eula Mae's bed.

She introduces us. "Gabriella and I have had such a good time getting to know each other."

"You've been exploring the river, Gabriella." Colonel Perkins stares at me.

"Yes, sir."

"It offers much of interest." He makes a light tapping motion with the flat of his hand against his hip.

Eula Mae invites me to come over again. "I very much want to hear more of your life experiences." She reaches for my hand. Her hand is warm.

No one's ever asked me to tell about my life before. Not anyone. Not ever.

"I promise, ma'am."

I take the tray of dishes to the kitchen and give them a good washing. I dry the things and put them exactly where I found them. Then I walk across the lawn to its edge so that I can look at the river below. There's a guy sitting on the beach with a guitar in his arms.

I plunge down to the beach and walk across the sand.

# Chapter 5
# Doyle and Emmett

I jump over pieces of driftwood and land at Doyle's side.

"Hey!" Doyle looks up at me with an easy smile. He lowers his eyes to the guitar once I've settled beside him. "I don't know entire songs yet. But I will soon."

"Well, anything will be fine."

I make sure I sit where I can watch his fingers on the strings and see the river, too. My legs are tucked underneath me to hide their hairiness. I'm not allowed to shave them yet.

Doyle strums the guitar.

It seems he touches all the strings just right so the notes sound clear. The wood of the instrument glows a deep warm brown in the sunset.

"You said stewards at the club are teaching you?"

"Clarence, mostly. And I'm learning from race records."

"What are they? I've never heard of such a thing."

He stops playing. "You don't hear them on the radio much because of the color of the musicians' skin. Sometimes Clarence tells me about things like that."

I stare at my hands folded in my lap. Then I'm looking at the river. The light of the sun shows red in the water, and I'm picturing the boy from my dream, the boy our teacher told us about. He's at the river with Hawkins. His name comes to me now.

His name is Emmett Till.

I figure as much as he knows about things, Doyle would have heard the name, and I ask him about Emmett.

He gives me a searching look. "What do you know about him, Gabriella?" There's a cautious tone in his voice.

I tell him the few things our teacher said about the murder. Also I describe a picture she showed us from when Emmett Till was alive. I see the photo clearly. "Emmett wears a hat, shirt and necktie. A person can see in the expression in his eyes and on his face that he was smart and kind."

"The men who murdered him weren't either of those things," Doyle says. He's looking directly at me. Then he tells what happened two years before now, in the early morning of August 28, 1955.

Doyle says that's when two white men kidnapped Emmett Till from his great-uncle's home near Money, Mississippi. One of the men learned that Emmett had wolf-whistled at his wife in the country store the couple operated.

The murderers pistol-whipped Emmett's head and face with .45 Colt pistols. They shot him in the head and tied a heavy cotton gin fan to his neck with barbed wire to weight him down. Then they rolled Emmett Till into the Tallahatchie River.

Three days later some boys who'd gone fishing found Emmett's mutilated body in the Tallahatchie.

"It was a lynching," Doyle says. "And all because a boy whistled at a white woman."

He shakes his head in sorrow over the horrible killing.

An all-white jury found the two men innocent of Emmett's murder. The men had admitted to the kidnapping, but a grand jury refused to indict them on that charge.

This whole time he's telling about Emmett's death, Doyle holds his guitar close. Every once in a while he looks at the instrument, like it's helping him tell what he knows.

There isn't anyone else around. But I swear there's a kind of solemn music rising from the river.

After I talk with Doyle and go back to my quarters, the general takes me to the officers' club to get some chow. We reach the club and one of the stewards tells him he has a telephone call. I race downstairs to the pool deck. I'd like to jump right in except I have on a dress with no swimsuit underneath. And my drawers are kind of in tatters.

I sit on the edge of the pool enjoying the feel of water sloshing around my legs. I can hardly believe what I'm overhearing. Two men at an umbrella table near me are talking about Emmett.

"The Till boy didn't have enough common sense not to flirt with a white woman."

"He hadn't gotten the word about how things are done down here," the second man says. "He was a northerner from Chicago."

The two men stand up and walk away laughing and talking. After they leave, I try picturing me swimming in all that shimmering pool water.

But I can't stop thinking about Emmett.

Upstairs the general's waiting for me at a table. When she's in a good mood, Mama likes to go out to eat. I mention to the general how much I think she'd like this club. He agrees with me, and I feel like it's okay to ask when she's coming home.

"I've said this before and I'll say it again. When I have something to tell you, I will. Now, we will talk of other things." His face is gray. I don't push him.

Instead, I ask if he knows the name Emmett Till.

The general's eagle eyes latch onto mine. His beaky nose suddenly looks more sharp than usual. "How do you know that name?"

"Well, sir, our teacher told the class about Emmett. Many others know about him, too."

The general sets his knife and fork aside. "You are too young to learn about the brutality of the world. You are too young to even try to understand."

Before I can stop myself, I shake my head no.

He sits back in dismay. "What? You're contradicting me?"

"Yes, sir. I'm too old to be ignorant as I am."

I want to tell him about the hard way the grown men downstairs beside the pool spoke of Emmett. Emmett was just a young person like me! I long for the general to say something about him. But he doesn't.

He looks past my left ear out the club window. If he had hair other than the bristles that pass for it in the Marines, he'd have run a hand through it. I think he doesn't know what to say to me.

He clears his throat and eyes my plate. "You are to eat your supper."

I make a show of spearing some food. But I don't eat anything. Much later, after I'm in bed, he stands in the doorway.

"Goodnight, Gabriella."

"Goodnight, sir."

He switches the overhead off in my room and starts to pull the door to. But he stops before he's closed the door entirely. He stands in a wedge of light from the hall. His figure is black with shadows.

"Nowadays in the Marines, all men, whether they are colored or white, live, train, and fight together. They die together fighting the enemy. Remember that, Gabriella."

"I will, sir."

He closes my door. I listen to him walk along the hallway to his room. His footsteps are heavy and slow. I climb from my bed and sit on the sturdy carton beside my window. At the edge of the lawn and below the steep slope, the river flows beneath waves of stars.

Soon Mama swims into my thoughts. Sometimes Mama doesn't get herself up until late, if she gets up at all. If she were here, I know she'd want to go for a walk along the river. Maybe she'd swim. It would help her, like it's helping me.

I think how I'd only spent a few hours with Eula Mae, but already she's a friend. Was it the wind or had she whispered the name "Jonas" as she gazed toward the river? Who is Jonas?

I think how I only know about Emmett Till through his death. I know nothing about his life except I saw the life in his eyes in the photo our teacher showed us. Is it possible for someone to become a friend when you know them only from a picture? Yes. I believe this magic happens.

One of the last things Emmett ever saw of this world was the Tallahatchie River in Mississippi. On its banks he'd known only blinding pain inflicted by his tormentors.

I want to walk with Emmett and show him that *this* river is a beautiful place.

I leave my place at the window and climb into bed. Outside the cicadas make the smooth dark rough with song. The restless sound of water rolls across the night. Then the river of sleep carries me away.

# Chapter 6
# Hawkins and Emmett

When I ask Hawkins what he knows about Emmett Till, the look on his face has me thinking of an ocean swell building before rolling to shore. Whatever's going on inside him, it's powerful. It might sweep me right along with it. We're at the river pool sitting on its small beach. Hawkins reaches into his shirt pocket for a pack of cigarettes. He taps one loose and lights it. This whole time he's staring at the river. He doesn't say anything at all. It seems like a lot of time goes by this way, with Hawkins dragging on the cigarette and staring at the river in silence. But then he begins talking about Emmett.

"He wasn't much older than you, Miss Gabriella. He was a boy." He turns his gaze from the river to me.

"But he was stronger than most men."

I ask Hawkins why he says this. Hawkins says that four months after they were found innocent, the two men described Emmett's murder in a *Look* magazine report.

"They kept beating Emmett, trying to make him afraid, trying to get him to say he wasn't as good as them. He never would say it. Finally they shot him through the head and rolled him into the river."

His arm rests across his knee with the cigarette held between his fingers. He stares at the burning tip for a long moment before flicking some ashes to the ground.

"So they couldn't torture him into saying he wasn't as good as them. Miss Gabriella, Emmett was fourteen years old, but he knew he was as good as them. He was strong and he was proud as any full-grown man."

I say to Hawkins that our teacher didn't tell us much. "But she said we must never forget Emmett Till."

Hawkins looks away from the cigarette and our eyes meet. "Your teacher's right. People need to know about his death. Maybe that knowledge will bring about some positive changes."

I ask Hawkins if he knows what the general meant when he said that all Marines train and fight, live and die together now.

"What did they used to do?"

"In World War II and before, a black man had to struggle for the right just to be able to serve our country in the wars. We were kept separate from white Marines. By the time I was shipped to Korea, no matter the color of a person's skin, Marines trained, lived, and fought together. We died together. Just like the general said."

"Is that the kind of change you were thinking of a moment ago when we were talking about Emmett?"

"Yes, ma'am, it is. Emmett's death may bring change to everyone in this country of ours. We have a long way to go."

"Well, what happened to change things with the Marines?"

"Change was coming, but it was slow. Then the war came along. And men were needed to fight in Korea. It didn't matter what color they were." Hawkins picks up his book, and I know I need to give him time for himself.

I slip into the water. Below the surface mermaids watch from hidden caves and from inside shifting shadows. Our teacher once told the class about the kingdom of Atlantis. It was peaceful and rich, she said. Its children had plenty of books, food, and friends to play with. Many artists and craftsmen, poets, writers, actors and musicians lived there. People from all different races and beliefs lived together in peace in Atlantis, she said.

My classmates gasped when our teacher told us that one day Atlantis was swept into the ocean. We felt somewhat better when she said that beneath the sea the mysterious lost kingdom of Atlantis became a special place of beauty for souls who've grievously suffered. In Atlantis they are made whole again, she said.

As I practice swimming, I pretend that centuries ago the lost kingdom washed from the ocean into the river and that I'll find Atlantis before the summer is over. Emmett might be in Atlantis. If he is, I'll ask him to show me around.

After my swim I'm walking home through the woods when Eula Mae's young neighbor Caitlin jumps out at me from behind a tree. She yells and waves stubby arms over her head.

"A bogeyman's gonna drown the general's daughter."

"I have a name. It's Gabriella Winter. The man who's teaching me to swim is called Hawkins."

Her brother, B.J., hops out from the bushes. "He's nothing but a big old bogeyman," B.J. shouts.

"He's gonna hold you under," Caitlin screams.

They follow me through the woods, screaming pretty much what they've already said, and by the time I reach our back porch stairs, I've had enough. I whirl around to face them.

"Calling Hawkins a bogeyman is childish and ignorant."

Caitlin stuffs a piece of candy in her mouth. She opens a grubby fist and lets its wrapper fall on our lawn. "I'm not a child. I'm ten and B.J.'s nine."

I step closer to them and scoop up the wrapper. "Hawkins is a Marine just like your daddy."

"He's not like our daddy!" Caitlin's eyes widen with shock.

B.J. waves his hand in the air. "You're gonna get punished!"

"Yeah," Caitlin says. "Punished real bad."

It could go on like this for a long time unless I get these children thinking about something else. I open the screen door and look back over my shoulder at them. Before making an offer of ice cream, I glimpse a red Chevrolet turning into their driveway. Caitlin and B.J. exchange worried looks and run home.

# Chapter 7
# To Be Like a Marine

There's a pot of wilted flowers by the door. Next to the flowers, some newspapers are stacked on the welcome mat. Trish and her family aren't back yet from their trip out west. I walk across the traffic circle to the general's quarters. I wish it wasn't such a big house. Inside, stacks of cardboard boxes greet me. They're still taped shut from the move here. I don't know how I'll explain it when Trish comes over after her vacation.

The general's talking on the telephone in his study about being available to meet someone named Miss Peder. I want to hear more, but just then the windows rattle as fighter jets slam into the sky and helicopters churn the clouds.

Hawkins told me about how it used to be with black and white Marines and how it is now. I want to see whatever I can for myself. I can't exactly sashay into a barrack, but I can do the next best thing. I need my bike, though.

The garage smells of gasoline, mothballs, dirt, and gardenias from the bushes growing near. I free my bike from a mountain of Mama's suitcases and boxes. I wheel the bike to the driveway, hop on, and pedal through the base.

Along the way I pass the white-painted officers' club with its stiff collar of shrubs. I hear laughter and the sound of splashing and the thump of the diving board at the pool. In the distance, jets and helicopters are parked at the airfield near its gigantic hangars. The life of the base is over there and at the rifle range.

Near the airfield I slow to a stop, jump off, and straddle the bike. I'm on a treeless dusty road staring at Marines marching close by. Beneath their helmets, their faces are in shadow. But through the dust kicked up by their heavy boots, through the shadows, I can tell that some of the men are dark-skinned, some are milk-white, many are shades in between. There are cut lips and freckles and at least one black eye.

From the bones in my feet clear to the tangled hair on top of my head, I feel the ground shake from the tramp of the Marines' boots. The hard music of their leader's shouted cadences sings in my blood. As they go by, I'd like to march along with the men.

They march so close together and they're all dressed the same, so it almost seems like they're one body. If a single Marine starts to fall, the others would likely scoop him up––take up his arms and legs and just carry him smartly along without missing a step. Sweeping by in their brown-green uniforms, they make me think of the river.

The Marines march into the distance. Where they had been a moment ago, columns of heat like a ghost platoon rise fierce and proud from the ground. I stand at the side of the road thinking how in a war they stick together like brothers, helping each other.

Marching through my veins is the hope that maybe one day I could in some way be like those Marine warriors.

Heading back to our quarters, I cruise by Trish's place to check it out again. The newspapers sit untouched on the welcome mat and the flowers still droop. The curtains are pulled to and the garage door is shut.

I jump my bike up and over the low curb of the traffic circle and roll down the curb on the other side.

As I ride across the street, a woman I've never seen before walks out our front door.

# Chapter 8
# Housekeepers

Miss Peder is unhappy with the job, and she hasn't even worked a full day yet. "All those clothes in the closet upstairs need washing. It's a disgrace."

I introduce myself. She says, "You tell your father I usually work in *fine big* homes with large staffs."

"Bigger than this?"

"This place is *not at all* big. And it lacks *fine furnishings.* It is *quite* common and *very dusty.* Moreover, you have just one servant." She presses her lips together to show distaste.

She views the house I live in as ordinary even though it's got an upstairs and downstairs and an enormous yard. And a steward waits on us. But according to Miss Peder, we practically live in a dump. I don't run over and hug her. But I come close to it.

⁂

Eula Mae listens to me complain about having the housekeeper around. Miss Peder hasn't started telling me what to do yet, but it's only a matter of time. Eula Mae doesn't offer sympathy. Just a few prickly words.

She adds a shot from the flask to her tea. "It is time for you to consider the situation from perspectives other than your own."

I shift uncomfortably in my chair.

"The general wants a clean house and clean clothes. He wants you to have an enjoyable summer free of care. And he wants another woman around to look out for you."

She finishes the tea and settles against her pillows.

I'm bristling at the suggestion I can't take care of myself. In a year I'll be thirteen.

"I found her sitting at Mama's dressing table. She wasn't doing any cleaning. She was just staring at herself in the mirror."

"What was the expression on her face?"

I have to think this over. "Like there wasn't a thing in this world to make her happy."

"Doesn't that say something to you about her? Doesn't it stir your sympathy?"

Eula Mae's forcing me to see Miss Peder in something other than a bad light. I cross my arms over my chest. I stare at the floor.

"You want others to see your good qualities and overlook the bad, don't you?"

"Yes, ma'am." I run down my list of flaws, wondering which ones she's thinking about.

She grips my hand. "Think also of Hawkins." Her eyes find mine. "A white girl in that house alone and him living not two feet away? Someone with evil in their heart might use you as a way to hurt him."

Now, suddenly, I'm thinking about the white woman who'd said Emmett Till had whistled at her. Emmett had been murdered because of it. But it just doesn't seem likely that someone might hurt Hawkins because of me.

Eula Mae's eyes are fluttering closed. She releases my hand and turns her head toward the window and the river beyond. When the colonel appears at her door, it's time for me to go.

Upstairs in my room I'm taking a late afternoon nap when I overhear Hawkins and the general talking. They are standing on the kitchen steps below the bedroom window.

The general offers Hawkins a cigarette. The two men light up. The general looks at Hawkins.

"Let me make sure I understand. Miss Peder the housekeeper accused you of stealing some silver from this house."

"That's right, sir."

The general studies his shoes and clears his throat. "In my experience, Marines don't steal silver."

Hawkins nods agreement.

At that moment, attack jets scream across the sky. The general and Hawkins, both combat veterans, drag on their cigarettes, watching. The deadly aircraft are gone in a heartbeat.

Marines don't steal silver. They kill the enemy.

After a moment, Hawkins says, "There's something else, sir. Miss Peder's cleaning needs supervision. I expected her to be more thorough."

"I will speak with her."

Miss Peder is a goner.

Maybe I should've thanked her for ending my worry that our quarters are too grand. Telling her that very thing might've uncorked some of her personal sourness. It might have made her a nicer person. Then she wouldn't be in the fix she's in now.

Several days later Miss Ward, another housekeeper, starts work at our quarters.

She's an older lady with a big body that makes me think of a water heater. She brings movie and romance magazines to share with me as well as candy.

I let her give me a permanent. Fortunately Trish returns from vacation right about then and knocks on our door. This is her first time inside our quarters. She doesn't even notice the unopened boxes stacked everywhere from the move to Rock Point from California. What she comments on is my hair.

"It's a mess."

"I know it."

We use the general's razor to hack away at the frizz. Miss Ward doesn't complain about all her work going to waste when she sees my new ragged look. Instead she hugs me and tells me I'm pretty. Then she dabs some of her thick red lipstick on me. I pucker my lips and stare for a long time at myself in the bathroom mirror.

Miss Ward's with us more than a month. She makes popcorn with melted butter and tells me stories about traveling with her boyfriend, Wayne, a long-distance hauler. She gives Trish and me manicures. For a few hours afterwards, my short nails look decent and ladylike with red polish. She brings me a heart-shaped pillow to lean against when we watch television together. I fall asleep sometimes with the pillow in my arms and my head resting against her shoulder.

One day she comes to work wearing a ring as glittery as anything from the five and dime store. Miss Ward pulls me to her side in a hug, leans down, and kisses my cheek. The ring and her traveling around the country on Wayne's eighteen-wheeler excite me, and I smile and look up at her just as she says to the general, "If I could, I'd take this child with me."

"You're not my mother." My voice is thick with anger, and I pull away from her. I'm about to run upstairs, but the general sets a hand on my shoulder and holds me in place.

"You will say a proper farewell to Miss Ward," the general orders. I mumble something through my tears.

Without looking at me she shakes the general's hand and hurries to her car. He goes to his study. I'm alone and thinking about stepping onto the front stoop, slamming the screen door behind me, and yelling, *"Go on now, just go away, Miss Ward, and don't you ever come back, because I won't be here."* But it's just as strong in me to run to her and bury my face against her big warm body. I'd say, *"Please come back, Miss Ward, oh please don't leave me."* Why don't I go to her before it's too late? She *has* been like a mother to me. I didn't mean what I said.

My arms hug my chest as I stand behind the screen door and watch Miss Ward drive away. She doesn't wave or look back. To chase away thoughts on how badly I behaved, I run next door to Eula Mae's.

There's no wind today, and the lace curtains in her bedroom hang straight as ghosts with good manners. So when I hear "Jonas," I'm sure it's her saying it. I want to find out who Jonas is and why she calls his name.

# Chapter 9
# Eula Mae's Story

I sit beside Eula Mae's bed and ask about Jonas. She pours from her flask into a teacup before settling against her pillows. Her cheeks are pink, her eyes bright.

Jonas and Eula Mae were both born in 1867, after the Civil War ended.

"My family owned a large estate in Virginia called Brightfields. Jonas was the son of former slaves at the estate." Eula Mae and Jonas were allowed to play together.

"We used to ride a horse named Star. She was very old. Jonas and I adored her."

The two children decided Star's real home wasn't in the barn but at the river. "That's where we spent our days. We built a fort at the river." Eula Mae brought books to the fort. She taught Jonas to read.

"We'd ride Star to the river. We'd play on the shore and read in our fort."

"One day Star died." Eula Mae turns to look out the window. "But we both knew she would come for Jonas and for me one day. She'd carry us to an enchanted land across the river." She returns her gaze to me. "We'd all be together again."

Not long after Star died, Eula Mae's father and Jonas's father tore the fort apart and ripped the pages from the books. The men told the children that they could never meet again.

"'You're not right in the head, boy,' Jonas's father screamed. He struck his son and kicked him so hard Jonas fell to the ground. My father dragged me to the house where I was locked in my room. The next day my family sent me hundreds of miles away to live with relatives. We were about your age. Our great sin was our friendship."

"Did you ever see Jonas again?"

She touches my hand. "No and yes. I have had three husbands. But Jonas is the one person I still see in dreams."

Star had died and Jonas and Eula Mae never saw one another after that terrible day. Still, I ask if she felt that any good had come from the suffering she described.

"I am forgetful now, but I will never forget him. Our friendship still gives me happiness and strength to go on living. And so in a way he has brought you to me."

On a sudden gust, the lace curtains rear in the window. Eula Mae's face shines with sudden joy. Then she reaches for my hand and holds it until she falls asleep nestled against the pillows.

I'm about to tiptoe from the room when I'm startled to see the colonel standing at the bedroom door. I wonder how long he's been there. So as not to wake her, he signals that I'm to follow him.

I wash and dry the tea things in the kitchen and meet him on the porch. He opens the screen door and steps ahead of me into the yard.

"There's something you should know about Mother."

"Yes, Colonel?"

"Mother likes to talk about a colored boy named Jonas. I must ask that you tell her not to speak of him and that you never repeat to anyone what she has already said."

"But why?"

"Mother has an active imagination. Jonas is one of its products." He brings his hand against his thigh with a light tap.

I don't know how to respond to the colonel. There's just no way I'd ever tell Eula Mae to basically shut up.

"Do you understand me?" He thrusts his face toward mine.

I step back.

"I understand, sir, that talking about the boy Jonas gives your mother great comfort. As her loving son you do want that for her, don't you? Well, sir, of course you do."

The colonel glares as I give him my sweetest smile before turning away and walking across the dry grass to our quarters.

# Chapter 10
# A Mysterious Phone Call

Each time the telephone rings, I think it's Mama calling to say she's coming home. She *has* to come home so we can string Japanese lanterns with lights around the backyard and have a party. July 4 is almost here. This evening when the phone rings I dash downstairs to answer it in the general's study. I just know she's calling me.

"Hello?"

I listen for her beautiful voice. But there's only a sound like waves breaking on the shore. I say hello a couple more times.

"Who is it?" I tap my foot. "Answer me!" I speak somewhere between loud and very loud. Then I switch from demanding to begging. "Mama, please answer. And say you're coming home now!"

I need her to tell the general to let me stay at Rock Point when fall comes. No more boarding school for girls. After doing a certain amount of time even convicts are set free!

With a hiss the connection breaks off. I hang up the telephone, switch on a light, and sit at the general's desk. When she calls the next time, I know she'll say to me, *"Darlin', oh I do miss you so."*

I think back to the day the general told me I was going away to school. Mama was in her room with the shades pulled. When he talked about my going to boarding school, the general glanced at the closed door to her room.

"It's for the best, Gabriella," he said. He gazed into my eyes. Then he looked away.

"Sir, what do you mean 'for the best'?"

I remember him walking toward Mama's closed door and standing there with his head bowed, like he was thinking how to say something. When he walked back to me he said, "If she knows you're in a good school learning and making friends, your mother won't have so many things to worry her. Away at school, Gabriella, you will have the opportunity to improve your mind, body and spirit. Millions of people never have that opportunity."

The general said I needed to be in a "better academic environment" than some of the schools I'd been to already. But I suspected the real reason for being sent off was that as far as he was concerned, I hadn't done a good enough job looking after Mama when he was away.

At boarding school they said I needed to improve pretty much everything about myself. I wasn't good enough at anything. I'm thinking back to this while sitting in the general's study gazing at the telephone, waiting for Mama to call again. I try concentrating to make the telephone ring.

A framed photograph of Mama sits next to the phone on the general's desk. The bunched up front of my T-shirt makes a good cleaning rag to wipe the glass free of fingerprints. Leaning close, I try looking in her eyes.

But no matter which way I turn the picture, she gazes right past me. It seems like whatever she's looking for it's somewhere out in space. It's not here on earth. It's not me she's looking for.

I think about her with tears in my throat. If the general isn't around and she takes to her bed, who'll brush her wavy mermaid hair and soothe her? I won't be able to if the general sends me off to school again in the fall. She needs to come home and explain everything to him.

A gust of wind circles the room with a sound like whispered secrets. A scrap of paper sails off his desk. I grab the paper from the floor. The writing on it looks like some kind of foreign language until I see I'm holding it upside down. When I turn it the right way, I recognize the general's handwriting. He's written the word "Bellrive M." What does this mean?

"Bellrive M." I whisper it while switching the lamp off. It feels like I'd just found a secret code for contacting aliens. Outside the window, fireflies search the black ocean of night for small lost things.

A car pulls up in front. Its door opens and closes. Then the general steps past the front screen door. I go to meet him.

We are in the hallway. There are more lines in his weathered face and they seem deeper in the hallway's harsh overhead light. His shoulders appear to sag. Looking up at him is like seeing one of those old statues in a park that's beginning to lean and crack. I tell myself it's only the poor light.

He clears his throat. "Gabriella," he says, "your orders are to fix us dishes of chocolate ice cream with plenty of that canned syrup you put in your milk. Make it snappy."

"Yes, sir."

We eat sitting on the back porch with its view of the river below. Once he's tucked away some of his dish of ice cream, it seems to me like the general's in a good enough mood that I can mention July 4 and ask about Mama. There's no telling exactly what he might come out and say in an unguarded moment when he's full up with chocolate ice cream and syrup.

"Sir, when Mama comes to Rock Point..." I don't get to finish.

"This is not a matter that a young girl need concern herself with. When the time is right, she will come back."

"Yes, sir."

"She will, Gabriella." His eyes meet mine. They are red-rimmed. The circles beneath his eyes are darker than I've ever seen them.

Beyond the porch screen and the tall pines, the river flows wide and dark. On its far shore, there's a building where a few early lights glitter. They're like the diamond earrings from the dime store I helped Mama pick out one time. I've never seen her wear them.

❧

Well, July 4 is finally here. The day whirls by with marching bands and booming fireworks. But what I long to see are lighted Japanese lanterns strung between pine trees and beneath them, Mama and the general dancing.

# Chapter 11
# War Story at the River

I go looking for Hawkins and find him downriver from his usual spot. He's sitting on a log with a book propped on his knee. When he sees me walking toward him he closes the book. I sit cross-legged next to him. I'm noticing a crease from the side of his nostril to the corner of his mouth. If I sit forward just a little, I'm able to see an almost identical crease on the other side of his nose. The crease is partly erased by the long line of his scar. The creases and scar make him appear old.

He sees me studying him. "What is it, Miss Gabriella?"

"You're old but not like the general. You don't have gray hair or bags under your eyes like he has."

"Young lady, I may not be old in years but I feel it sometimes. I'll turn twenty-eight soon."

We fall silent. There's a small breeze, and the cooling shade offers some relief from the damp heat. Dragonflies hover over the river. He reaches for his book. I want to delay his return to its pages. I know his age now, but not much else about him.

"When did you join the Marines?" I snatch the question out of the air after watching three helicopters fly over.

"Seven years ago in 1950." He pauses. "I was sent to Korea."

The general spent time in Korea, but he won't say word one about it. At least not to me. So I ask Hawkins what it was like. He reaches into his shirt pocket and removes a pack of cigarettes. He taps one end of the pack on the side of his hand so that a cigarette slides forward.

"I've never been so cold in my life. It was the worst cold I ever felt."

"Were you ever scared over there?"

"Yes, ma'am. You'd have to be living on another planet not to be scared every now and then."

He lights his cigarette and releases a puff of smoke. The smoke curls and vanishes in the breeze. Hawkins looks over at me. "What else would you like to know?"

I grab a handful of sandy soil, letting it fall between my fingers. "Something else about the war?"

"Here's a story I can tell you. There was this man named Burt. We were walking with other Marines along an icy road, and Burt was telling me about how his parents were dead, he'd lost his job, and his girlfriend had run off without leaving an address. Suddenly, all hell broke loose around us. With Burt's luck, naturally he was closest to all the shooting. But neither one of us should've gotten out alive what with so many bullets flying around."

Hawkins tells me that Burt kept right on walking. "It was just a matter of seconds before he'd take a bullet." So Hawkins tackled him, and they both rolled into a snowy ditch.

"It felt like I was in that ditch for hours even though the firefight lasted only minutes. But tackling Burt meant I got to hear more of his story once all the shooting stopped and we were back on our feet. Burt told me that whenever pain stalks him, he gets busy dreaming up a song. Love songs. After that day I never saw him again. But I like to think he's somewhere still making up love songs. Without the pain."

Hawkins gazes across the river. Then he picks up his book. The way his eyes go right to the page he'd marked I know there'll be no more stories of Korea. I walk into the river.

Where we are now, there's this sturdy limb growing from a big old tree hanging out over the water. I grab hold of the limb, use it to swing myself up into the tree and make a shallow dive. Two more times I dive from the tree into the river.

Preparing for my last dive, I reach up and grab the limb. Right away I feel my bathing suit straps give way. I look down. I'm naked from the waist up. I let go of the limb and clutch the swimsuit top to my chest. On my way straight down into the water, I glimpse Hawkins.

His head's bent over his book. I'm thinking about all those sisters of his. I'm certain he couldn't have grown up in that family without seeing lots of naked chests. But, it's *my* bare naked chest he might've seen, and I briefly consider staying underwater for the rest of my life.

Instead I tie the straps behind my neck and with my lungs bursting, I rocket to the surface. Hawkins is gathering his book, bucket, and fishing pole. A cigarette dangles from between his lips.

I wrap the towel I'd stashed nearby around my shoulders and pull it closed in case the straps come undone. On our way through the woods, I chat about the swim meet.

"You're ready for it, Miss Gabriella. But you should familiarize yourself with the club pool so you'll feel comfortable at the event."

"There's time for that."

"Take advantage of it then, young lady."

I can tell by his manner he didn't see me when the suit top headed south. I don't give it another thought.

Back home Trish calls and we agree to go to the club pool. I ask for a loaner bathing suit. She has several she's outgrown. She'll bring one that should fit me.

At the club pool's locker room we change into our suits. The one she brought for me is probably from when she was in fourth grade. Just like she said, it fits me. I mention that most of the summer is gone, and I still have nothing that could be called hips and my chest is still flat. I admit that I want to hear from her that things will soon change for the better.

Trish pops her gum and fastens the straps of her suit. "What you just said about your hips and chest? That's all true."

Well, but something important *has* changed in my life: I'm a swimmer now. Didn't Hawkins just say

I'm ready for the swim meet? He also said I need to be more familiar with the pool.

I challenge Trish to a race.

# Chapter 12
# Underwater Flips

"Race *you?*" Trish almost laughs in my face as she looks me over. I'm staring at her. "Well?" I lift my chin. She shakes her head, indicating the hopelessness of my challenge. After flashing a confident smile and snapping her gum, she says, "Okay, let's go." We prance across the sizzling hot deck, jump in, and swim the length of the pool. The whole time I keep in mind all that Hawkins has been teaching me. He'll be interested that the race ends with me only about two lengths behind Trish.

At the deep end we fold our arms on the pool edge. I'm looking into the water when I feel her eyes on me.

"What are you looking at?"

"You're not as scrawny as you were when I first met you. Don't ask me why I'm just noticing this now."

I tell her that swimming has helped me. "But I've got more practicing to do."

"You must've spent every day while I was gone here at the pool. Or were you at that creepy place on the river?" Her eyes glitter like pool water.

"I was here. And at the river. It's not a creepy place, Trish. Why not come with me sometime?"

"I like the pool. Come on. I'll show you something that'll help you compete."

"You're sure you want to do that?"

"I'm sure. Having real competition makes me swim better."

We head toward the shallow end. When we get there I listen to Trish's instructions. "I'll swim across the width of the pool. You go to the side where I'll come in. Get there before I do. Then watch what I do as I reach the wall. I'll do it a couple times so you'll get the idea."

I'm standing above her on the deck when she reaches the wall. I see her flip over and turn underwater like she's doing a somersault. Then Trish pushes off from the wall with her feet. Her arms are straight out in front of her as she angles upward to the surface and continues swimming the crawl.

After practicing, I find the unbroken swimming loop she just showed me means I don't waste time or energy on unnecessary moves. We race the length of the pool to the deep end and to the shallow end once more.

When I reach the wall, Trish is already on the ladder climbing out.

"I've got to go home." I'm puzzled by this since we have the pool practically to ourselves now. She's staring toward the deep end and the man speeding toward us through the water like a torpedo.

At first I think it's Hawkins. Then I see the man is taller and heavier than he is. At the wall he does a flip and turns, pushes off, and rockets away.

"He sure is good!"

"He *is* good."

I follow her to the locker room where we pull on our shorts and tops. Trish says, "I've seen colored men clean pools. I've never seen them *in* a swimming pool before now."

"Well, it could be he's an officer. Let's ask him."

"Nope, not me." She stuffs her suit in a bag. "Why do you think he's an officer?"

"You have to be one or an officer's family member or guest to swim at the officer's club," I remind her.

We're climbing the concrete stairway that leads to the street and officers' quarters. I look back at the pool. The swimmer is walking toward the men's locker room. For just a moment he pauses and stares at the empty pool. Then he's gone.

Jets roar from the airfield and howl overhead. Helicopter rotors beat against the sky. We don't even try to talk as we walk home.

At her quarters, Trish invites me in. We fix glasses of lemonade and settle on her back porch. A large copper-colored dog appears from inside the house. The dog hops up on the couch and sits between us. His tongue lolls. His breath is warm on my cheek.

"Hugo, get down," Trish orders. The dog lifts his ears and wags his feathery tail. But he doesn't budge.

"So much for obedience," Trish says. She smiles at Hugo. It's clear this dog can do no wrong.

I rest my cheek against his big head. It's a peaceful feeling, being close to the old dog. I hug him and Hugo smiles. I'll swear to it.

We finish our lemonade. On the way to the front door, Trish takes a sharp left and disappears along a hallway. When she returns she's carrying two large grocery bags. Frilly collars and sashes hang out of the bags.

"I'll carry this one, you carry the other." Trish pushes a bag into my arms.

I peer inside. "Your clothes that you don't want?"

She looks away from me. "Mom thought you could use a few things I can't fit into anymore."

We cut through the traffic circle and cross the front lawn of the general's quarters. Its shadow wraps around me like a cape that's too big, too long, and way too heavy. Trish holds the screen door partway open while I set my bag aside and take the other from her.

"At the pool? Thanks for showing me the flip turn and push-off." I close the door.

She's standing on the front stoop peering at me through the screen. I don't invite her in. I don't thank her for the clothes. My thanks might make her smile from the good deed her mother had done in helping me. I don't want to see that.

My back's to her as I move to the steps and start to climb. I hear her call my name.

"Gabriella?"

I pause, turning toward her so that I have half a chance of hearing through a window-rattling roar from the airfield.

"If you don't find anything you like, give those things away or toss them. Just please don't bring anything back. Mom will start letting seams out and remaking everything."

"Okay." I ask if she wants me to return the swimsuit she lent me.

She tells me to keep it.

"There's something in one of the bags that goes with it." Trish pops her gum and gives a small smile. I watch her jog across the street wondering what she's up to. Then I hurry with the bags to my room and dump the clothes on my bed.

There's a handwritten note with the clothing: "Dear Gabriella," the note begins, "I hope some of these lightly used things will fit you. How is your beautiful mother? Someone thought she might be staying in a place across the river from us. If you have the address, I'd like to send a nice card. Or if you think a visit would help, I'll drive us all there. We could take her a nice lunch and have a picnic by the river!"

It's signed by Trish's mother, Betty Smith.

I've only just glanced at the clothes, so I don't understand why there's this knot of anger in my chest. But I'm thinking, *Why isn't Mama here? She'd take me shopping! She'd buy me pretty things that are new! I just know she would.*

I set the note on the bed and begin pawing through the clothes. By standing on a chair I can see myself in the dresser mirror. Some outfits don't work. But denim pants, shorts, a skirt and blouse look good. I reach in the second bag and pull out a navy-blue T-shirt. Its color perfectly matches the swimsuit she's just given me. It's plain and unremarkable, like my friendship with its former owner. And I'm thinking it's the most wonderful shirt I've ever owned.

# Chapter 13
# "Ragged and Dirty"

Doyle shows up one evening at our back porch. "Hey, I just learned a whole song from start to finish. Want to hear it?" I tell him of course I do, and I open the door and step outside to sit on the porch stairs. He settles cross-legged on the grass before carefully lifting his guitar from its carrying case. The last colors of the sun sink down into the river.

"First I'll do a warm-up." Doyle's hand brushes the strings. He plays some chords I recognize from a popular tune.

"Elvis is great," I tell him.

"There are unknowns just as great. Elvis learned from them. Colored musicians. Listen to this."

His fingers move across the strings. When he finishes, he tells me, "That's called 'Ragged and Dirty'. It's by a man named Willie Brown. What do you think?"

It kind of shocks me to hear being ragged and dirty as the subject of a song. Also I'm startled at being asked my opinion. I sit and ponder all this for a minute.

I tell him, "The song's different from what I'm used to. But you played and sang great."

He's looking over at me, and I can tell he hopes to hear more. I take a second to decide. "I like it."

The back porch steps are across from Hawkins's quarters. There's a light burning outside his front door. I wonder if he's ever heard the song Doyle just played and if Emmett ever listened to it. One thing I know: Emmett was never "ragged and dirty." The picture our teacher showed us was of a youth in a pressed shirt wearing a necktie and hat. He looked real sharp.

What Doyle just played isn't like the music I sometimes hear coming from the radio in the kitchen. Once when a piano tune was playing, I'd asked Hawkins what it was when he'd come into the dining room with a pitcher of water. He told me that particular piece was by a fellow named Chopin.

I ask Doyle if he wants something to drink. He nods as he strums, and I go inside where I fix us glasses of iced tea. Willie Brown's song dances right along beside me into the kitchen. Thinking it over, it seems to me that song isn't just about someone needing a good wash and mended clothes. It's about wanting to be close to another human and finding a home. When I bring him his tea I tell Doyle this. He gives me a long look and he says, "That, too." He moves from sitting on the grass to one step down from me.

The cicadas sing like they're trying to tell the whole world about being alive. Fireflies float through the trees. I like it that Doyle's come over to sing and play for me.

When we finish our tea, Doyle walks with me beneath the pines to Eula Mae's.

"I'm learning a couple more songs," he says. He moves his guitar case from one hand to the other. "Maybe I could play them for you sometime?"

"Well sure. I'd like that just fine."

Doyle looks off into the night, but not before I see his grin.

Soon we're at Eula Mae's door, and I knock. Doyle's hand touches mine, but he's standing so close I figure it's just an accident. I hear the colonel's footsteps coming toward me. Doyle and I say goodnight, and I watch him walk beneath the pines until the colonel holds the door open. I step inside wishing our talks weren't so uncomfortable. He gives me a sideways glance from his eyes that always look too big for their sockets.

"Mother's been asking for you."

"I don't want to wear out my welcome, sir. I was here earlier."

"She thinks of you as the granddaughter she never had."

I can hardly believe he's saying such gentle things to me.

"Thank you for telling me and for calling to invite me over even though it's kind of late." We're standing in the dim hall outside Eula Mae's room. I'm thinking that maybe the colonel and I can get along after all.

"The other day I saw that steward from your quarters walking along the river. He carried a book."

"His name's Hawkins, sir. And yes, Hawkins always has a book with him. A fishing pole, too, but he hasn't had much luck with that."

“Oh? Really?” He gives me what I think is a smile except it’s tight as strung wire. His lips look like they might snap.

In Eula Mae’s room I carry the chair I always sit in to her bedside. “There you are,” she says. Her voice is thick with sleep. “Tell me about your day.”

I tell her Doyle played guitar for me, and I describe the music. “I’ve never heard anything like it before. I can’t even hum it.”

Eula Mae looks so very small and pale. I know it’s late for her to be up. We talk a little more and then it’s time for me to go. She presses my hand, and I breathe her scent of lavender. “Goodnight,” I whisper.

I walk toward home, the dry grass crunching beneath my sandals. Something’s shaking the bushes behind me, and my heart jumps. My legs turn to jelly. Over by the general’s quarters a long shadow moves in the driveway. The shadow moves toward the stewards’ quarters beyond the garage. Of course it’s Hawkins.

I call to him.

He hears me though it seems to me like I’ve barely spoken his name. He walks swiftly across the yard. We meet midway beneath the pines, and I tell him I’d heard something. We both listen. The rustling sound has stopped. With Hawkins beside me I sure don’t feel scared anymore. The pines bend and sigh in the night wind. Above the river, the full moon is a golden fish swimming near an island of cloud.

I glance at Hawkins. The scar on his face is a winding band of silver. We walk, and it’s like swimming beside him in the trembling sea of night.

The stars are big in the sky.

# Chapter 14
# Trouble at the River

It's overcast, and when the breeze dies the damp heat and mosquitoes are obnoxious. I haven't forgotten my promise to Hawkins that I'd never go in the water alone. But I jump in anyway to cool off and make myself less of a target for insects. All I see is a zigzag movement as the snake swims by about four feet from the tip of my nose. It appears to be minding its business, but I sure don't want it deciding to get friendly. So I hop out of the river fast. There's a sound of twigs snapping. The bushes part, and Caitlin and B.J. make faces at me from the riverbank.

Caitlin steps onto the sandy beach. "So where's the bogeyman that's teaching you to swim?" She pushes sweaty hair off her plump face.

B.J. follows his sister. "Yeah, where's he at?"

"That warty monster's gonna pull you under." Caitlin grins. Melted chocolate sticks to her teeth and lips, and I about laugh at the sight of her. But she'd be furious.

"Why on earth would Hawkins want to drown me?"

The two children exchange a glance. "Because he's colored."

If anyone were to ask me which would be worse, drowning, getting warts, or being around Caitlin and B.J., my answer would not involve warts or drowning.

Caitlin finishes her candy bar. She's wiping her hands on her shorts while I take a closer look at the two of them. Their faces and clothes are dirty, but what's more important, they both look miserable. Suddenly I'm thinking of the happiness I saw in Emmett's eyes in that photo our teacher showed us.

If Emmett knew what was going on here, I think he'd want someone to help these children get away from name-calling. He'd want them to grow up to be decent human beings. Others being good to them will help.

It comes to me that I hadn't seen either Caitlin or B.J. in the officers' club pool. They could need lessons like I did. And I don't believe they've ever met Hawkins.

"Caitlin and B.J., I've got an idea I want to share with you." They give me doubtful looks, but finally they both come closer to me. "I'd like to get to know you better, spend some time with you. What about the three of us going on a picnic? We could meet at my quarters and walk here together. I'll bring the food." I don't say this to the children, but what I'll do is tell Hawkins my plan so he can be here.

Caitlin presses her lips in a tight line and folds her arms across her chest. "Nope, can't do that."

"River's off limits," B.J. says.

"But you're both at the river right this very minute."

The brother and sister exchange worried glances. "It's okay because you're here and, you know, you're kind of old," Caitlin says.

It seems likely their parents have given them strict orders about playing in the woods at the river, so naturally they can't resist. "If someone finds out you were here you won't be punished if you were with someone older?"

They hold a whispered conversation. "Yeah," says Caitlin.

"That's great. I'll be with you, so you can come on a picnic, right?"

Caitlin punches B.J. on the arm and the two of them agree to the idea and a day and time. Then they run up the footpath. I collect my towel, shorts, and shirt and trot behind them. We reach Hawkins's cottage together.

Both Caitlin and B.J. stare in the direction of their house. The red Chevrolet is parked in the driveway.

"He's home already." Caitlin's face goes white. "Quick, B.J., think of something to tell him."

"We were with the general's old daughter. I mean Gabriella."

They take off toward their quarters.

❧

After they've gone, I walk around the side of Hawkins's cottage and find Doyle waiting for me on the porch steps. "Hey there, let's go to the river."

"Well sure."

We walk across the lawn between the pines, Doyle carrying the guitar in its case.

When we reach the beach we sit cross-legged in the sand. I ask to hear the song he played before called "Ragged and Dirty."

When he's done he sets the guitar to one side and leans back, resting his weight on his elbows. His muscles show under the sleeves of his T-shirt. Our eyes meet, and then we both look at the river, neither of us saying anything.

There's a bright flash of light on the opposite shore.

"What's over there?"

"The little town of Bellriver."

What I've just seen is the sun reflecting off the windows of a large red brick building with what appear to be white columns in front. I'm squinting at the building when I see Doyle, shirtless and with his pants rolled up to just below his knees, walking into the water.

He calls to me, "You going to come on in?"

I jump up and follow. We let the river carry us along the shore a little ways. Then Doyle splashes me. It isn't a real big splash, more like a friendly swell in the same way his easy smile grows across his tanned face.

We slosh out of the water and stand dripping onto the warm sand. All summer I'd noticed a tang of salt in the water and in the air, and I ask Doyle about it now.

"The river's a mix of rain and salt water driven upriver from the ocean," he says. Doyle dries himself with his shirt and, careful not to get it wet, sets his guitar in its case. We climb the slope. Halfway to the lawn we stop to look back. The wind's off the river, and I taste its salty sweetness on my lips.

# Chapter 15
# Atlantis

Hawkins's arms are folded before him on a table. His head's bent over an open book, its pages splashed with yellow light from a small lamp. I knock at his door. The chair he's sitting in makes a little scraping sound as he pushes away from the table. He steps outside, closing the screen door behind him.

"Good evening, Miss Gabriella. Can I get you something to eat or drink?"

I look down at the concrete path leading from his quarters to the kitchen. *Please let me stay with you a little while. I promise not to be a bother.*

"Could I have a glass of water?"

Hawkins steps inside. He returns carrying a glass of water with ice. He hands me the glass, and we walk together beneath the tall pines to the edge of the lawn. The sun's setting on the big river below.

"What were you reading just now?"

"I've been studying the plays of William Shakespeare for a test." He pauses. "The test is tonight. I don't feel ready."

A sudden worry has me in its grip. Once Hawkins passes the test, he might go away from here. The hope that he wouldn't pass finds its way into a mean corner of my brain. I look out over the river in silence. I'm too ashamed to speak.

When I do, it's to ask him a question I didn't even know I'd been thinking about.

"Where's your home?"

The colors of the setting sun rest on his shoulders like a cloak. The scar on his cheek is a warrior's ribbon. I swear I hear him say, *I'm from Atlantis.* I think back to our class when we learned from the teacher about the ancient Greek kingdom with that name. Atlantis is at the bottom of the sea.

Hawkins is saying, "A man can live a good life in Atlanta."

*Atlanta.*

Atlanta is his home. I'd never pictured him living anywhere other than in the stewards' quarters next to the garage. But the little building where he lives now isn't his real home.

"When I've fulfilled my obligation with the Corps, Miss Gabriella, I'm going to open a restaurant in Atlanta. It will be known as the finest in the city." He rubs his hands together in anticipation.

"You'll invite me to it, and you'll sit at the table and eat with me?" If he says yes, then I'll have something I can hold onto and imagine.

"Yes, ma'am. You'll be my honored guest."

I'm already thinking about being with Hawkins at his restaurant. What I refuse to think about is Hawkins ever leaving here.

The sharp sound of a horn has us both looking toward the driveway behind us where a car I don't recognize has pulled in.

"There's someone I want you to meet."

Hawkins guides me to the driver's-side window. "Gabriella, meet Katherine Johnson," he says introducing me to the beautiful stranger behind the wheel. Hawkins leaves us to step inside his quarters.

"Hello, Gabriella." Katherine holds out a hand with the prettiest long, red-painted fingernails. I clasp her hand with its jewel-like nails in my sweaty paw. Her skin is warm brown like Hawkins's, but her eyes are green.

*Katherine, please show me how to wear color on my cheeks and if you have any extra time, could you help me find a bra? I'm pretty sure I'm going to need one sometime in my life.*

"Would you like to come in? Mama is away and the general isn't home, but I can fix you some tea, hot or cold."

"That's a fine invitation." She glances at her wristwatch. "But I'm afraid we'll have to do it another time. We're driving to the school over in Bellriver."

"The town across the river? I see lights from this big old place over there at night and when the sun shines on its windows."

"I think I know what it is." Katherine opens the car door and steps onto the driveway. We walk a short distance across the lawn. Katherine points to the far side of the river. Behind some pines the mansion comes into view. It has white columns.

"That's Bellriver Manor you've been seeing. I work for the people staying there. The town is called Bellriver."

The note that fluttered to the floor in the general's study spelled Bellrive M. in his handwriting. And Trish's mom wrote in the note to me she thought Mama was staying across the river.

Katherine's green eyes search my face. "Gabriella Winter. What a lovely name." She turns her head slowly to gaze at the mansion. "If you are ever over that way, it would be a pleasure to see you, Gabriella. Please stop by."

She fixes me with her eyes and repeats, "Bellriver Manor. You'll remember the name won't you?"

"I will."

Just then Hawkins leaves the stewards' quarters. I return with Katherine to the car.

Hawkins climbs into the passenger's seat, his arms loaded with books. Katherine slides behind the wheel. They call good-bye to me, and I watch until the car's red taillights disappear. They are driving to the base gate and out to the big world.

Fireflies with their light and cicadas with their song make the evening jump. The pines dance in the rising wind. Below the edge of the lawn, the river moves restlessly.

On the porch steps of the general's quarters, I sit with my shoulders hunched and my hands twisting together. Hawkins has a beautiful girlfriend. He has a home away from here. And I, Gabriella, am a monster circling beneath the surface of the river, scheming to make Hawkins mine.

Mine alone.

The name Atlantis comes to me from somewhere in the wind. Suddenly I'm floating over rooftops, swimming through flooded streets and palace rooms in the kingdom of Atlantis. I'm looking for Emmett. I just know he's here. When I find him I'll turn into a mermaid. We'll swim together through hidden passageways and mysterious caves. We'll listen to music and dance. Mostly, I know Emmett will get me laughing. Just from seeing his lively eyes and his smile, I know this about Emmett. But what do I have to give? I want to give Emmett something.

On the shore opposite Rock Point, the brick mansion where Katherine works glitters like a palace in the lost kingdom of Atlantis. Something's drawing me to that place, something powerful as the moon pulling the tides.

# Chapter 16
# Doyle and Me

One moment I'm sitting on the back porch steps chomping a blade of dried grass and feeling like a monster. Next, I'm staring in astonishment at a young man standing at the foot of the steps. Actually, I'm staring at his head. It's shorn like a Marine's, which means he's close to bald.

Doyle gives a crooked smile. "Dad insists on a summer cut."

"Well, you don't need hair to play guitar. Why didn't you bring it with you?"

The words are hardly out of my mouth and Doyle's racing across the yard to his quarters to fetch the instrument. I'm thinking about how I'll listen to one or two of his new songs. After that I'll make an excuse and go inside, leaving him to head home. I want to be alone. It's because I still feel wretched from scheming to keep Hawkins for myself.

Then Doyle's crossing the lawn. He's carrying his guitar in one hand and in the other a plate covered in foil.

"Mom just made these." He hands over the plate and sits beside me. With the covering foil off, the sight and scent of chocolate chip cookies has me just about swooning.

Maybe it's the nearness of another human. Or listening to music and talking with someone. There's a good possibility it's the food. Whatever, I no longer feel like a warty old monster.

And now that I have a guest to look after, I'm no longer giving all my attention to the light above Hawkins's door. I belong right here on the porch steps with Doyle beside me. He's playing his guitar. For me.

"A penny for your thoughts." Doyle gives me a sideways glance.

"That's a puny sum." I tilt my head, snobby-like. Doyle laughs.

"How about we go to the club for Cokes? Playing guitar makes me thirsty."

My skirt has a salad oil stain on it, and I think about changing into something else. But it's dark out now, and the stain probably won't show.

He sets his guitar inside our porch, and we walk to the club. Soon we are at the concrete steps that lead to the pool. The steps are next to the formal dining room and ballroom, and we can hear a band playing inside. A big picture window shows the dining room's crowded for the weekly buffet and dance. Everyone's dressed in their finest. The picture window also overlooks the pool, deck, and snack bar.

We hurry down the steps. Someone has already put a bunch of coins in the jukebox. Doyle buys us Cokes, and we sit on the rim of the swimming pool listening to the music and sipping our drinks. Our legs dangle in the water. The water's so bright and still, it looks like it might break into millions of pieces if anyone jumped in.

I think about Mama and the full-skirted dress she'd let me pick out for her to wear one time to a dance, flowers pinned in her mermaid hair. I think of the gardenia perfume she always wears.

"As soon as she comes to Rock Point, Mama and I are going shopping. She'll want a new dress and so will I." I'm picturing all the ladies upstairs dressed in their finest clothes. "She can't take me shopping just now, though. She's busy with other things." These last few words slip out as a whisper, and I steal a quick glance at Doyle. I'm worried that I've said far too much about my family.

I feel his eyes on me. He doesn't ask where she is or what she's busy doing or when she'd be coming to the base.

"I know." Doyle says this in a way that tells me he heard something in my voice beyond what I just told him about shopping and Mama. He listens to me in the same careful way that Eula Mae and Hawkins listen. I feel stronger for this.

As we sit at the edge of the glittering pool the wind starts. It picks up little waves for the music to dance with. The band upstairs finishes one song and starts playing the 1955 hit called "Unchained Melody." The jukebox is silent for now.

"I think I'll try that song on my guitar."

"You know I'll want to listen to it when you feel it's ready."

"Let's write down the words. Between us, I bet we can remember all of them."

Doyle grabs my hand and helps me from the water's edge. All the way across the deck he holds my hand. He doesn't let go on the concrete stairs leading away from the pool. We walk up the stairs, pausing and leaning on the metal railing every so often to listen to the band play "Unchained Melody." Well, it's just a long and beautiful song.

In near total darkness we walk along a winding road. We both stop to look up at a military cargo plane, its navigation lights flashing as it drones overhead. Doyle's lips brush mine, and I feel a small shiver, like wind touching flowers in a field. We stand there peering at each other through the blackness. Then we're chasing one another, shouting, "Wait for me, wait for me!" Our laughter and the chorus of cicadas rise and whirl with the unchained stars.

# Chapter 17
# River Kids

I just can't ignore any longer the tug I feel from those lights on the opposite shore. Trish's mom said in her note she thought Mama was staying somewhere across the river. Katherine invited me to Bellriver Manor. And there was the scrap of paper falling from the general's desk. The letters on the paper match the Bellriver name except the 'r' is missing. From all this it's clear Bellriver is where I'm supposed to go. I'm thinking it should be easy to get there since I can see the manor from the Rock Point side of the river. But I might end up lost trying to find it on my bike. So how to get over there is vexing me.

I'm ankle-deep in the slope's sandy soil. Doyle's already on the beach. I race across the hot sand.

"Hey." Doyle looks up at me with a smile, and I drop down beside him. Immediately I tell him where I want to go and my worry about getting lost. He plays a chord on his guitar. "We can row to Bellriver."

"Well, you need a boat to do that."

He points along the beach. "Look over there. The river's already brought us one."

Pieces of wood are missing from the old row-boat. But it's got a pair of oars, and when we shove it into the water, it doesn't sink. It even has a name: *Mermaid*.

We push and pull it up onto the beach so it won't float away while he goes to his quarters to leave the guitar and let his mom know where he's going. Birds wheel and cry overhead. On the far shore I see kids jumping into the big river. I'm eager to be over there already.

Doyle comes back with news. "Mom wants me to help her with some things around the house. How about we go tomorrow?"

"Of course," I tell him. But something inside's urging me to make the trip now.

I watch Doyle climb the slope to the lawn. He reaches it, turns toward me, and waves. Since the night of our kiss, the night of "Unchained Melody," I've thought how I'd like this to happen again sometime. I wave back.

When I no longer see him, I step into the old boat and settle on its seat. My mind circles the unknown. On my own can I row across the big river? Can I even push the boat into the water? I'm strong from Hawkins teaching me to swim. I'm determined not to say, "Can't." But right this moment I'm a little worried about reaching my goal. Also, I'm hungry.

I head back to the general's quarters. As I rattle around in the kitchen fixing iced tea and a peanut butter and grape jelly sandwich, Trish calls through the open kitchen window.

"Gabriella, you there?"

Above the whir and click of the metal fan and water running in the sink, I holler for her to come in. Soon she's stepping past the swinging door that leads into the kitchen. She's hungry, too, so I'm fixing extra sandwiches for her. I tell her I'm going by boat to search for Mama in the town of Bellriver.

"Come on. You've got to be kidding." Trish stares at me in disbelief as she takes the gum from her mouth and helps herself to potato chips from a bag on the counter. "What makes you think she's over there?"

I tell Trish about the note to me that her own mother included with the old clothes she gave me. "There've been a few other clues. But mostly, well, it just feels like a tide's pulling me over there."

"Oh, brother." Trish rolls her eyes. "You're going to Bellriver because 'a tide's pulling me over there.' Sounds crazy."

My hand that's holding a knife to make sandwiches with pauses above a piece of bread. The knife's coated with grape jelly. I stare sideways at her.

"I'm crazy for trying to find Mama?" I should stop talking right about now. But I don't.

"Well, Trish, maybe you're the crazy one for being scared when we saw Hawkins at the river. And then you were upset over the man we saw at the pool who was just a terrific swimmer." I slam the blade of the knife down and slice into a piece of bread. I meant to use the knife to slather the bread with jelly.

"What are you talking about?" Trish's voice is cold as the ice in our tea.

"I thought you were going to turn tail and run when we first saw Hawkins."

I'm about to set the sandwiches and chips on plates when I feel a puff of air on the backs of my legs. It's the kitchen door swinging open and closed. I peer over my shoulder. Trish is gone.

Through the kitchen window I watch her run between the tall pines in our yard and across the traffic circle. The trees are like bars shutting us off from each other.

❧

Trish had scoffed at the idea, but as I row across the river, I feel an invisible force drawing me toward Bellriver. She'd called me crazy. It's a common enough expression so that I'm not upset with her anymore. But I'd insulted and hurt Trish by suggesting that she was a coward; I didn't actually use that word, but she got my meaning. Nobody wants to hear something like that about themselves, military brats especially. With an ache I wonder if we'd ever be friends again. For now, though, I have other things to think about. I'm a combination of excited over this trip and exhausted from getting the boat back in the water all by myself and now rowing it. The opposite shore is further away than it seems.

By the time I land on the opposite shore my clothes are soaked with sweat and river water. So I pull off my shirt and step out of my shorts. Underneath, I'm wearing Trish's bathing suit, the one she loaned to me and then let me have for keeps. I kick off my sandals and step into the shallow water.

An older girl sitting nearby watches young people and little kids swim and ride inner-tube rafts on the river.

Now she's looking me over. "The swimming pool's in town." Her skin is the brown of iced coffee.

"Why should I go there?"

"It's the pool for white folks. I hear they got showers and mirrors." She looks away from me.

"I like the river. I swim in it about every day."

She has nothing to say to this.

Up a gently rising lawn, I glimpse an enormous red brick building. Its wraparound porch is perfect for nestling in a chair with a book during a thunderstorm. There are white columns and stone steps leading to the front door. There are many windows.

When I've looked from the Rock Point side to this shore, I've seen its windows flash with light. I'm almost a hundred percent certain this is Bellriver Manor where Katherine works. But I don't want to go traipsing in there unless it's the right place. I ask the girl.

She lifts her shoulders in dismay at my ignorance. "Everybody around here knows what that place is. Where you from?"

"The base."

She gives me a long look.

"Rock Point? That's kind of far to row for someone skinny as you."

"Well, I have an important mission." I introduce myself and ask her name.

"Delia." Then she tells me the building's known by local folks as the old O'Hara mansion. "It's called Bellriver Manor now."

"The O'Hara family doesn't live there anymore?"

"You sure ask a lot of questions." She glances away from me, and I think she's going to clam up. Instead she turns to me with more information.

"The O'Hara family is dead and gone. A whole lot of people with different names live there now from time to time. They all have troubles. That's what brought them here."

"What kind of troubles?"

"Some sit in their room just staring or sleeping. Some cry. There's some that holler and slam stuff around. Others try to wander. You have to keep an eye on every one of these folks. I work in the kitchen."

"That's got to be hard. Especially in this heat."

She shrugs. "You get used to it."

I'm cooled off from the heat of my trip. I like talking with Delia, but I need to remember what brought me here. I pull on my shorts and shirt.

"I thought you were going in the water," Delia says.

I feel like I've failed her in some way. "Delia, I think my mama's in Bellriver. I need to find out."

"That's your mission?"

"Yes, it is."

"I understand," she says, her voice soft.

Suddenly she's jumped up and she's at the water's edge yelling at a youngster to come closer to shore. I watch him scramble toward Delia.

I take a moment to watch the children. Beads of water mix with sunlight on their wet skin. Emmett's out there with the youngsters. He rides along with them in the currents, dives with them to explore the river's kingdoms. Emmett's laughing with the children. I know he'll guide them safely home.

# Chapter 18
# In an Old Mansion

I leave the river behind to climb Bellriver Manor's steps and walk between its white columns. The cool dark draws me inside. At the end of a hallway, a woman is speaking on a telephone. I reach her side and find myself staring into green eyes. Katherine Johnson hangs up the phone.

"Miss Gabriella, it's good to see you again."

Right away I'm thinking of Hawkins. I'm staring at Katherine like my eyes are frozen in my skull. Monsters like me are known for making scary awful sounds in their throats. So I'm afraid to even try saying, "Hello." Still I want to touch her hand with its lovely painted nails. I want to wear her perfume. I'm torn between jealousy and longing.

I force myself not to think about Hawkins. Instead, I ask Katherine my question.

"Is Maria Winter staying here?"

"We can't give out patients' names. But some of them will be down shortly for tea in the visiting room. Why don't you stay?"

Sunlight and flowers fill the room where she leads me. There are upholstered chairs, a long couch, and a square table set for tea and coffee. I fill a napkin with cookies and take a seat off to one side.

I'm not sure what I expected, but it isn't the frightened look on a young woman's face, the fixed grin an older man wears like a flower pinned on his lapel, a woman poking at every single thing on the table and naming it. There are whispered words, the clink of spoons, a harsh laugh that's way too long and with a shriek in it. The wind streams through open windows.

Mama comes into the room with Katherine at her side. Katherine goes to the tea table while Mama walks with uncertain steps to a nearby armchair. She doesn't look around. She doesn't see me. She sits with her head bowed. The last time I saw her was in the spring. She had some color in her face then. Now she is too pale. She is too thin.

Katherine sets a cup of tea on a table and stands beside her. "Your daughter's here, Mrs. Winter."

Mama grips the chair arms and raises a bewildered face to Katherine. "Honey, what did you just say? I can't have heard you right." She's still looking up at Katherine, waiting for her to say words she can understand instead of what she's just told her.

Katherine's brown fingers adjust a sweater over the gray-green dress Mama wears. "Your daughter, Gabriella, is here to see you."

Mama shakes her head. "I told her daddy that child is never to be allowed to visit. I *told* him that when I decided to come here."

So the general's only been following her orders, and she doesn't want me around. I'd just heard her say it. At this moment I close my heart to Mama. Why, then, do I find myself walking over to her?

"Don't blame him. He doesn't know I've come to visit you."

She jerks her head toward me. In the eyes that travel over my face, I see a light so distant I can't hope to reach it. *Hawkins says I must never say can't.*

"Mama, I've thought about you all summer." My throat tightens. "I want you to tell me you'll come home. If not now, then soon."

Her chair is beside a window with a view of the river. She turns her head toward the water.

"Then the both of us might drown," she whispers.

Waves of emotion wash through me. "There'll be no drowning," I tell her, "not now, not ever. I can swim almost as good as you. When you come to Rock Point, you'll see."

Her mouth trembles.

I am strong. Hawkins expects this of me.

"I can't go there, darlin'. I'm not ready."

If I could get her to laugh like she used to, she'd want to come home. She'd listen to the radio with me instead of keeping to her room. She'd fix my hair like Lucille Ward had tried doing. Mama would only have to try once and my hair would come out perfect.

"Do you remember when we ran out of gas and we just sat there laughing until that man in the truck came along?"

She gives me a blank stare "Honey, I don't remember. I don't remember much of anything."

She lifts a thin hand, lets it fall to her lap, bows her head. I reach out and push a strand of dark hair behind her ear and off her cheek.

"Listen to the sounds out there on the river. They're laughing and having good times riding rafts and swimming. Mama, we can do that."

She balls a hand into a fist and brings it down on the chair arm. She doesn't hear the children. She hears something else.

"Lies. That's all they ever do is tell lies about me. Out there somewhere." Her face twists with sudden fury.

"Don't go making up any more invisible enemies! There are enough visible ones to wear everybody out." I scold her like she's my daughter and I'm the mama.

She looks sideways at me, fixes me with a long stare.

"You wouldn't know anything about it," she says, her voice full of anger.

"Well, I sure do know it's time you start working on improving your mind, body, and spirit instead of locking yourself in a dark room. You'd better come home soon, Mama, and behave yourself."

She draws in her breath, lets it out. She reaches up to touch my cheek. "Oh honey, you can be so hard."

A little distance from the mansion and off to one side, a neglected half-empty swimming pool waits for children and young people to make it beautiful again. Beyond some large trees at the edge of the lawn the river tosses spears of sunlight to the sky. Rock Point is on the other side of the river.

We're both looking at the river as fighter jets thunder over. "Your daddy comes to see me. He brings me flowers."

I remember one time after Mama had kissed him on his weathered cheek, the general set the tips of his fingers on that exact spot where she'd left a red lipstick mark. His face filled with wonder. It was as if he'd been kissed by an enchanted being.

She has black hair and skin the color of cream. I look at her and think, *She came here from Atlantis.*

Mama's saying, "It's gonna be night soon. You'd best go home. Go on, now, darlin'. This is no place for you."

"I'll be back." But the words stick in my throat like small broken bones.

Mama stares outside. The moon's rising above the river. She points to it and says, "Oh, just look at that, honey." I love her for this. I put my arms around her shoulders and rest my cheek on her hair. Emmett is by the river. He's comforting a tearful child.

I walk with her to her room. She curls on her bed so that she faces a wall. I say a quick prayer to St. Agatha, the patron saint of my boarding school: *Please let her walk with me by the river. Let her come home soon.*

On my way out I meet Katherine. And it seems that Mama has a friend I didn't know about until now. Katherine sets her hands on my shoulders and looks in my eyes. "You'll come visit again?"

"Yes, ma'am, I'll do that."

"Girls need their mamas. And mamas need their girls."

It seems I have a friend I didn't know about either. Until now.

Outside I look for Delia and the children. They've left the beach. I look for the *Mermaid.* In the distance I see the little boat I'd rowed to this place. The boat and its ghost passengers are continuing their travels down the river.

# Chapter 19
# Sharky's

By the time I figure out I should've asked Katherine for directions from Bellriver to Rock Point, I've gone too far to turn back. My stomach growls as the odor of fried food draws me up the steps, across the sagging porch, and to the door of Sharky's Restaurant Bar and Dancing.

Inside, wooden tables are crowded together. There's a dance floor and in one corner, a man strums a guitar and another encourages sweet notes from a harmonica. The music has a familiar sound to it, a little like some of the tunes Doyle plays for me. At the back of the room, rows of glasses and bottles sit on shelves behind a bar.

I stand outside the doorway looking in. It isn't direct, but all the same I know I'm being watched. I'm a stranger here. Just as I'm about to go on my way, an enormous man in a clean white apron rolls away from the bar and walks toward me. Streams of smoke escape the cigar clamped between his teeth. He removes the cigar.

"Miss, can I help you?"

"Yes, sir. I need to get to Rock Point Marine Base."

He nods and smiles. "Old Sharky, he'll do what he can to make that happen."

"Now Sharky, we sure don't want the po-lice to have an excuse to come in here," a thin woman calls from a table nearby.

Sharky turns on her. "You shut your mouth, sister."

Heat rises in my face. What had I been thinking coming here? I'm about to run when a meaty hand grips my arm, and Sharky half carries me to a table.

"Can't I sit outside?"

"Girl, you sit where I'm telling you to sit." He pulls out a chair and pushes me into it. A cloud of steam and the clatter of dishes escape from the kitchen as Sharky disappears inside.

He returns with a platter heaped with French fries, hot buttered biscuits, and deviled crab cakes. Puffing on the cigar, he pours Coke into a frosted glass, topping it off with a doll-size red paper parasol. Dessert is a thick slice of pecan pie with whipped cream.

Couples are dancing. Maybe the day will come when I'll wear a pretty dress, someone will hold me close, and we'll sway to music the whole night. With a fast number, the dancers swing into action. They jump and spin, their bodies shaking all over.

I set my fork into a second piece of pie when the door opens and a man enters. Heads turn. People shout greetings. They reach out to shake his hand as if he was royalty. They touch his arm. He walks tall, a king among men.

I slide down in my chair, hoping the king won't see me. But he steps to my side.

"Take your time, Miss Gabriella. Then you and I will drive to Rock Point."

Moments later I climb in the front seat of Hawkins's car. As he slides behind the wheel, I smell salt wind and shoe polish. I sit very straight. I feel shy sitting near Hawkins in the dark.

With the window down and the evening pressing warm against my skin, I think briefly about the mystery of a man and a woman alone together. Of course I know something about this from Miss Ward's romance magazines. But right now it's too overwhelming to try to remember any details.

Hawkins glances across the seat at me just as he might, I tell myself, if it was Katherine sitting beside him and they were on a date.

I feel a sharp twist of jealousy. *Katherine sitting beside Hawkins in the car.* I turn from him and stare through the passenger window into the blackness. I'm ragged and dirty from my boat trip to Bellriver and my long walk. And I'm so young. I feel awful because there's something else I keep thinking about: how I'm still scheming to snatch Hawkins away from her even though Katherine's my friend now.

"Am I at all like Katherine?" My voice is small with worry about what he might say. I think I've shocked Hawkins into silence with my bold question.

"You and Katherine are the finest ladies I know," Hawkins says. Just then the fine lady scratches a mosquito bite on her upper arm. Hawkins keeps his eyes on the road.

*I am a fine lady.* I sail clear out of the car on waves of light sprinkled with stardust, the little parasol presented to me by Mr. Sharky clasped in my sweaty hand. I'm flying in a big loop around the Milky Way when Hawkins's voice brings me tumbling back to earth.

"Miss Gabriella, are you going to tell me the story of how you came to be so far away from Rock Point?"

Oh no. He'll lecture me now for sure. "Mama's staying over in Bellriver at the place Katherine works at."

"Yes, ma'am," Hawkins says. I can't tell if this is the first he's heard of it or if he knew already that Mama's at Bellriver Manor. I'm not sure it matters.

"Katherine will take good care of her."

"There's this pool at Bellriver. If it was all cleaned up she could go in that pool and swim. It would help her."

Then I tell him what he maybe already knows. "But she's too sad for swimming right now."

The kind of quietness you find in a chapel settles in the car.

"You just keep on being yourself and loving her." Hawkins grips the steering wheel and glances sideways at me.

"Yes, sir." I don't say anything for a moment. "But sometimes I don't feel much love for her. Like today."

Hawkins considers this. "That's why I think you're a warrior as well as a fine lady, Miss Gabriella."

"A warrior?"

Hawkins nods. "Because you keep trying to understand and make things better, even when you find they aren't easy."

He returns his attention to the road. We're both silent until I begin telling him something I hadn't told him before. "I had to learn to swim so the general will see I can be really good at something. He'll be proud, and he won't send me away again. And I can help Mama."

"What was that you just said?" Hawkins gives me a sharp glance.

"If I can show the general how good a swimmer I am, he won't send me to St. Agatha's boarding school. He'll be proud to have me at home."

"Hold on a minute," Hawkins says. "I don't know what your daddy may have told you. But I know the general's *already* proud of you."

"What makes you say that?"

"Because I know you and I know the general. I also know that like some others who have been through a lot, he's just not one for saying or showing much of what he feels."

I wish I could figure out what the general had gone through to make him silent most of the time. I'll try to listen better when he does say something. I start to tell this to Hawkins, but he's peering into the rear-view mirror. I turn around in the seat and follow the direction of his glance.

A vehicle with a flashing light and wailing siren's closing in on us.

# Chapter 20
# The Sheriff and Hawkins

"Git out of the car, boy." The sheriff is all leather and chewing gum, his face pocked as a waffle iron. Hawkins opens the car door and steps onto the road. I start to slide across the seat after him. But he frowns at me over his big shoulder. He shakes his head slightly, and I know I'm to stay in the car. Hawkins and the sheriff stand near the car door, though. I can hear and see everything.

"Where y'all headed?" The sheriff shines his flashlight at the license plate.

"Rock Point Marine Base, sir. Miss Gabriella Winter and I both live there. I work for her father, General Winter."

"Is that right?" The sheriff sounds as if he believes what Hawkins just said about as much as he believes in the Tooth Fairy.

Hawkins pulls his wallet from a back pocket and offers a bunch of identification cards. "Here's verification, sir."

The sheriff grabs the cards and runs his flashlight beam over them. When he's done he shoves them at Hawkins in such a way that some of the identification falls from his hand and scatters on the ground. Hawkins bends down to collect the cards. He glances at the sheriff while he does this. It happens fast, the sheriff using the toe of his boot to kick some of the ID cards around.

Hawkins collects the remaining cards, straightens, and stares at the man, unblinking.

The sheriff glances at his wristwatch. He's avoiding Hawkins's gaze.

"So you expect me to believe you both live on the base and you work for her daddy?"

"I just showed you the evidence, sir."

The sheriff rakes the beam of the flashlight over Hawkins from head to toe. "That don't explain what the hell a colored boy's doing with a little white girl snuggled up close." He walks to the car and shoves his face toward me.

I'm tempted to slap his ugly mug, but I catch sight of Hawkins. The expression in his eyes warns me to be careful.

The wind sighs through the pines on either side of the country road. There's not another car around, and the sheriff has a gun. He can do whatever he wants to Hawkins. *Like those murderers did to Emmett Till.*

"Did you have something to say, missy?"

I slide forward and set my feet on the road, but I'm still sitting in the car.

"I went to Bellriver to visit someone. I got lost on my way back." I tell him about Hawkins coming to get me because the general, my father, is in Washington, D.C. now. "He's seeing our president."

"Well, how about that," the sheriff says. He spits something thick and yellow into the beam of the headlight.

"Hawkins is the general's most trusted aide." I hang onto the steering wheel to stop myself from shaking so bad.

"See that scar on his face? He got that in a war saving lives. He won't tell you about it, though, 'cause that's how he is. Hawkins is not a man who talks about himself much." It feels right. All of it.

"I'll bet he got that scar from a knife fight over a woman in a bar. I'll bet a pig farm on it."

I bolt from the seat and stand in the road.

Hawkins voice is a growling whisper. "Miss Gabriella, you need to stay inside the car."

I follow Hawkins's orders.

The sheriff pats the handcuffs dangling at his side. "I have half a mind to haul you two characters in for disturbing my coffee break."

He shines the flashlight toward the back seat. The light catches the edge of some clothing hanging from a hook near the door.

"Say, what's all that?"

Hawkins's Marine Corps uniform, pressed and fresh, with all its medals attached, glows beneath the zigzag of light.

The sheriff inspects the uniform and medals. He turns around and stares at Hawkins.

"I was in Korea, too, with the Army." He gazes across the highway into the trees. It's as if he's remembering the snow and the orange flash of rifle fire. "Me and my buddies almost died there. The Marines saved our butts."

The sheriff rubs his jaw with his hand. He waves the flashlight and directs such fearsome looks at Hawkins I feel sure he's going to smash Hawkins's face and then come after me.

"Go on, git back to Rock Point. I don't want to ever see either of you pitiful excuses for human beings around here again." The sheriff spits something nasty as he waves us on our way.

Hawkins rummages in his pocket for a handkerchief to wipe sweat from his face. He turns the key in the ignition. The motor springs to life, and we glide onto the road. The sheriff's car speeds off in the opposite direction.

I look at Hawkins. "The sheriff stopped us because of me." My eyes are beginning to fill.

Hawkins shakes his head.

"If it was Christmas Eve and Santa himself along with a couple of elves were sitting right beside me in the front seat, that sheriff would have stopped us." Hawkins adjusts the rearview mirror. "He was going to stop me no matter what."

I struggle against a growing army of tears.

He touches the scar on the side of his face. "Miss Gabriella, you made me sound like a hero."

I think how the sheriff just treated him. I think about Emmett's unspeakable suffering at the hands of his murderers for an innocent whistle. My heart feels as if it's breaking.

Suddenly I fling myself across the seat and press my wet face against Hawkins's arm. "No one should've ever hurt you." I don't need light to see the ragged scar.

"There now young lady. There, there." Hawkins awkwardly pats my hair. "The way you spoke up may have saved us both from spending the night in jail." He returns his hand to the steering wheel.

I sit up straight, grabbing a tissue from my pocket and blowing my nose. "You really do think so?"

"Yes, ma'am, I certainly do." He pauses. "A fighter might suffer setbacks, but she'll pick herself up and be even stronger than before." He glances at me. "And that's you, Miss Gabriella, just like I said. You're a fighter, a warrior."

I sit tall beside Hawkins.

We pass the dark silhouette of the train station. Rock Point is straight ahead. We stop at the red light of a railroad crossing, its alarm clanging. The sudden thunder and lights of an oncoming train punch holes in the night. Hawkins glances at the train racing by. He watches until the last railroad car disappears.

I'd travel anywhere with Hawkins.

I'd help him wash dishes. I'd go to the library and find a book that would show him how to catch a fish. I feel bad that to my knowledge he hadn't caught a single one so far. We'd take turns reading the fish book. We'd swim in the river.

At the general's quarters, I open the car door and hop out. Hawkins drives away. I don't know where he's going. I stand on the path and watch the taillights on his car grow dim.

# Chapter 21
# My Secret

Through the pines in our yard, I watch Trish going to and leaving her home. She never once looks toward my quarters. At the snack bar and pool she gazes past me without speaking. I don't make any effort toward her either. It's as though we're on opposite shores of the ocean. The water is rough, and I don't know how to get to her to say I miss her. Or if I even want to.

I tell this to Eula Mae. She pours a double shot from the silver flask in her teacup and rests against some pillows.

"You might call or drop by. She may hang up the telephone. She may slam the door in your face. However, if you want her friendship you must reach out. Only then will you find a way." Eula Mae sips from her cup. "But for heaven's sake, don't sit around fretting. Do something so you can learn from your experience."

Trish answers the bell on the first ring. She doesn't smile or invite me in, though. Clearly her feelings are still raw from my pretty much calling her a coward.

"The other day I said things I feel bad about. Trish, I want us to be friends again. What do you say?"

She shrugs and doesn't say anything. But she hasn't slammed the door. She looks in my eyes. "I want us to be friends again, too. But I feel I have to tell you, Gabriella Winter, that you're blind to danger. Reckless, even. The fact is, I have far more common sense than you do."

"I'm working on it."

"Not nearly fast enough."

She opens the door and I hustle inside before she has a chance to change her mind. We sit on the back porch with her dog Hugo hunkered down between us on the couch.

It's good being with her again, and I want to make the friendship closer. Because of this I consider telling about Sharky's and after that Hawkins's encounter with the sheriff as I rode with him to Rock Point. Then I think of the bathing suit incident at the river.

I turn to Trish. That's when Hugo presses a warm paw on the side of my leg and gives me this deep look. Trish says he needs to go out. I cross the porch and open the door.

His feathery tail drooping, head down and tongue lolling, Hugo lumbers off the couch. He finally rolls completely out the door, but with more than a few backward glances at me. Outside he plants himself on the grass and faces the part of the river you can see from Trish's quarters. Then he turns and stares at me.

I walk over to Hugo, a tennis ball in my hand. I toss it. He points at the river. Suddenly my blood goes cold. How could I have forgotten Emmett and the river? If anyone heard my bathing suit story, they'd decide that Hawkins probably *had* seen me half naked.

*Emmett only whistled at a white woman. They murdered him for it. Just like with Emmett's whistle, this story about Hawkins would spread all over the base and probably outside the gates, too, until someone felt that protecting my "honor" was their duty.*

The wind moves through the pines. Hugo stares at the river.

"Okay," I whisper. "I understand now." I return to the porch with Hugo at my side.

"Everything okay?" Trish asks.

"Yes, ma'am." I sit again on the couch near Trish with Hugo between us, the way things were earlier.

Only now I'm thinking these heavy thoughts. About secrets, about death. I decide that what happened when I was with Hawkins down by the river would go with me to my grave. It might be the best thing I ever do in my entire life, keeping this secret, even if I live to be old as the general.

Trish already knows I went across the river looking for Mama. It's why we got in a fight in the first place, my going over there. So I talk with Trish about her.

"It's not easy to talk about, but I found Mama. Trish, I don't think she'll be home real soon." I give her a direct look so she can see and feel the seriousness of what I'm telling her.

Trish slips an arm around my shoulders and gives me a quick hug.

"So who's going to go with you to buy your first bra? Who's going to show you how to shave those hairy legs of yours?" She snaps her gum. Her eyes are bright.

"Will you, Trish?"

We agree the time for a bra purchase hasn't quite arrived. But in the Smith family bathroom, and with Hugo's help, Trish introduces me to the mysteries of leg shaving.

# Chapter 22
# A Disobedient Daughter

I'm sitting in the study alongside the general's desk. His face is gray and solemn behind a haze of cigarette smoke. My stomach churns. My hands sweat. Why has he called me in to see him?

"Gabriella Louise Winter. You visited your mother the other day. Isn't that so?" His face is like the prow of a ship bearing down on me.

"Yes, sir, I did go see her."

I couldn't expect Mama to keep my visit a secret. But it had been a few days since I went to Bellriver, and the general hadn't said anything until now.

"You went to see your mother," he says again. "Who told you where to find her?" He drags on his cigarette, waiting.

"Nights before you come home I've seen lights across the river, and..."

"You are to tell me who told you, period. No frills. No wild stories." A muscle snaps in his jaw.

My throat is dry and I'm parched. "Yes, sir."

He flicks the ash from his cigarette into a small dish. "You may proceed."

"Well, sir, nobody said to me, 'This is where your mama is.' I just had a strong feeling about it because of the lights across the river. And it turns out I was right."

I don't tell the general about the note Trish's mom included with the used clothing, the scrap of paper on his desk with the name Bellrive M on it, and Katherine looking for a long time at Bellriver Manor and then at me, like she knew of some important connection. I don't tell him about meeting Delia and hearing about the guests there.

"Your mother says you were with her for most of one afternoon."

"Yes I was, sir. I was hoping she'd come home with me or give a date when she'd come home. And I wanted to cheer her up."

When I first stepped into his study, the general's face had been sharp with angles and lines. But as I tell him about Mama, his face sags. The circles under his eyes become darker than before.

He leans forward and folds his hands, prayer-like, on top of the green blotter on his desk. He stares into the middle distance of the room.

"Your mother needs rest." He pauses. "And then she will come home to us, Gabriella."

"Yes, sir. I understand that."

He gazes through the study window into the night. "In the future, you are not to spend a lot of time at Bellriver Manor. Your mother is delicate. She upsets easily."

"I know, sir."

"There will be no further discussion. The fact is you made an unauthorized visit. You went where you did not have express permission to go. You are thoughtless and disobedient." His words are harsh, but the muscle isn't snapping in his jaw anymore. More than anything, he seems exhausted. And though I'm here beside him, he seems all alone.

I climb the stairs. I'm relieved he didn't ask how I got myself across the river. He didn't ask how I got home, either. In my room I sit on the carton beside the window. The night is cool and I wrap a sheet around my shoulders. I can see the lights of Bellriver Manor glittering on the far shore.

Mama's over there. She's gazing at our quarters. Her mermaid hair's spread across her shoulders, and she's thinking of me. She loves me. I know she does. Had it really been so wrong to try to find her? The general had refused to talk with me about her. But he'd never once said for me not to go looking for her!

Come to think of it, as we were talking just now he hadn't come out and stated that I couldn't go see her anymore. In fact, he'd said I wasn't to spend *a lot of time* over there. That's not the same thing as saying, "You are not to go over there," which is what he might actually have meant. On this particular point, though, I won't ask him to explain himself.

I sit with the sheet around me and look at the night sky. I'm feeling calm at last about Mama. Then from below I hear Hawkins's footsteps along the driveway moving toward his quarters. Time slows. I picture the scar on Hawkins's face and his eyes that are the color of the river. I think of my bathing suit top falling away from my chest. Someone might know this. They might drag him from his bed, beat him, shoot him, and tie a heavy fan around his neck with barbed wire, then push him into the river.

Eula Mae had warned me to think of Hawkins. Instead, I may have brought danger to Hawkins's door. The thought is unbearable, of Emmett's body, of Hawkins's body, being pulled from the river.

Mama's okay but Hawkins may die because of me. High overhead, searchlights slide across the heavens like a skeleton's fingers, probing. There's the distant sound of gears and motors. Men and heavy machinery grind through the shadows. If I shout loud enough, wouldn't they rush to me with their lights and guns and root out whoever plans to hurt Hawkins?

The truth is I know the men are much too far away to hear me shout for help. Too far away to reach Hawkins with their machines and weapons to defend him from someone waiting to attack him in the dark.

Hawkins is at the door to his quarters now. I want to yell for him to watch out.

Too late, he steps inside. A light comes on. Music drifts from a radio, and I stop shaking.

Still wrapped tight in my sheet, I cross the bare wooden floor and climb onto my narrow metal-frame bed. For a long time I stare at the ceiling. It could be I'm losing my mind. Sometime later, I hear the general's steps on the stairs and in the hall. The footsteps stop outside my bedroom. In the slice of light beneath the door, I see the shadow of the general's shoes.

"Goodnight, Gabriella." He didn't say much, but I hear something low and hushed, like sadness, in his voice. His footsteps soon fade.

# Chapter 23
# "Hawkins is Not a Bogeyman"

Caitlin steps from inside her house onto the front stoop. She wears a big hat with a floppy brim. A little scarf is tied around her neck. I remind her today is the day we'd agreed on for the picnic. Her eyes shift away from mine. I sense she's going to say she and B.J. can't make it.

"Well, Caitlin, it sure looks like you're dressed for adventure. And there'll be cake."

"Okay. We'll meet you."

Around lunchtime, the brother and sister knock on the porch door. I grab the hamper of prepared food, and the three of us walk along the footpath through the woods to the river pool. In the near distance we see Hawkins fishing.

"Oh my gosh, it's that bogeyman. I mean that Marine." Caitlin stops on the path. It looks as if she might turn around and run off.

B.J. punches her arm. "There's food."

Hawkins waves as we push aside the bushes and troop across the sand.

I introduce everybody. Hawkins goes back to his fishing. B.J. retreats to watch from a distance before walking to Hawkins's side.

"What kind of fish do you catch here?"

"Bass, catfish mostly." Hawkins pulls on the line.

His saying this about what he catches has me almost falling to the ground laughing. In the whole time I've known Hawkins, I've never once seen him hook a fish.

Caitlin helps me unpack and set up lunch. B.J. soon joins us. I take a peanut butter and grape jelly sandwich to Hawkins. He eats over by the water's edge so he can keep an eye on his fishing line.

Suddenly all eyes are on Hawkins as he quickly sets his sandwich aside and almost in the same motion hauls in a large and lively fish.

"That's got to be a twenty pounder at least." B.J. looks from the fish to Hawkins and back again. His eyes are wide with admiration.

That catfish is beautiful, with long whiskers, sleek blackish brown skin, and a pretty white belly. Hawkins is quick to remove the hook from its mouth and release the fish into the water. It doesn't do anything for a minute. Everybody hovers, watching anxiously. Then it wiggles. We all sigh with relief as it swims off.

I hadn't expected Hawkins to let the fish go, so I'm glad when B.J. asks about it.

"Life is sweet in the river for a nice catfish like him," Hawkins says.

"Will you show me how to fish?" There's a greater hunger in B.J.'s voice than earlier when he'd asked for more sandwiches.

"I'd be happy to, young man."

"I want to learn to fish, too!" Caitlin elbows B.J. aside.

"I'll be happy to show the both of you what I know about fishing." I smile to myself, thinking how Hawkins must finally be doing something right to have caught such a big fish.

We all help ourselves to large hunks of chocolate cake. I'd made that, too. Then Hawkins has to leave to take care of some Marine business. We follow a little later, taking the path through the woods. The path ends at Hawkins's quarters.

"Well, I think we should have another picnic sometime," I tell them. They stare at the ground. Finally, they both look directly at me.

"Hawkins is not a bogeyman." Caitlin's eyes are thoughtful.

"He's a good man. A Marine." B.J. folds his arms across his chest.

"I thought you'd like him once you met him."

"We told our daddy about Hawkins."

Caitlin's news worries me. I can't let on, though. "What did you say to him?"

"We said a colored bogeyman lives next door to you. We told Daddy you called us childish and ignorant for saying Hawkins is a bogeyman."

B.J. chimes in. “We told Daddy you said Hawkins is a Marine same as him and that we got mad and said that’s not so.”

“Well, what did your daddy say to all that?”

“He said, ‘Gabriella is entirely correct.’”

B.J. punches his sister on the arm. “Then he grounded us a couple hours for being childish and ignorant.”

Still punching each other, the two head toward home as the red Chevrolet pulls into the driveway.

# Chapter 24
# Visitors From Across the River

The colonel has set a heap of blankets on Eula Mae, but her hands are cold. I try to warm them in mine. She wears her white hair unbraided and spread across her shoulders, like she might've worn it when she was a girl. She seems far away. Still, Eula Mae's eyes find mine.

I ask, "Eula Mae, ma'am, can I tell you my life events of the past few days?"

"Yes, dear, but you must speak slowly and clearly. And please open the window."

I do as she asks though I don't think opening the window is a great idea, and I draw my chair up close. I tell her how I invited Caitlin and B.J. on a picnic with Hawkins down by the river, and Hawkins taught them to fish. "They used to call him a bogeyman. Now they like Hawkins."

Eula Mae asks for something to drink. I fix tea and help her sit up. She's too weak to handle the silver flask, but it's easy enough for me to find. It's under a blanket. I pour a small amount from the flask into her cup. She sips deeply before leaning back on her pillows.

I tell her of meeting Hawkins's girlfriend, Katherine.

Eula Mae's eyes are closed. Her voice is faint. She says, "What's she like?"

"She's smart. Hawkins told me Katherine and I are both 'fine ladies.'"

I tell her about riding with Hawkins in his car after he found me at Sharky's and about the sheriff stopping us on our way to Rock Point.

"This happened after I went by rowboat to Bellriver and met Katherine at the place where she works."

I'm almost to the main parts about Mama, but Eula Mae's drifting off. I worry that I've overwhelmed her. I decide to go ahead and finish anyway. She might hear some of what's being said. So I tell about finding Mama and how I'd tried to open my heart to her, but I hadn't been able to as much as I wanted. I was angry at her.

Then something that had been on my mind a long time pops out. Is it possible, I ask Eula Mae, that I caused Mama's troubles? That this is why she and the general want me to go away? In their hearts, they see me as a troublemaker.

Eula Mae's eyes flutter open.

"Come here." Her voice is commanding even though it's frail. I stand up and lean in close. She manages to set her arms around my neck in a fierce embrace.

"Gabriella, whatever makes you think you are so powerful?"

I shake my head and hike my shoulders as she releases me. I don't know how to answer. I return to my chair.

"Do you think you can change her?" Her voice is growing more faint.

"No, ma'am."

"Then do not think that you are powerful enough to cause your mother's troubles." There's a sudden flash in her eyes. "Let that thought go."

For a moment I hold her hand tight as I can without bruising flesh or snapping bone. I press her hand against my cheek.

"Yes, ma'am. I will."

"Give her your love. Remember, she must do the rest."

It's growing late. I hear Colonel Perkins's footsteps along the dark hall.

Before leaving, I look at my friend. Her head's turned to the open window. The lace curtains, rustling and restless, prance into the room. And I hear the names Star and Jonas whispered in the wind.

"Goodnight, Eula Mae. I'll see you tomorrow."

# Chapter 25
# A Gift for Eula Mae

A brooding stillness settles on me as Colonel Perkins ushers me to a chair on the shadowed porch. "Is Eula Mae up yet?" I ask. On my way over here I was excited about giving my friend something I found at the river. But now I feel only the heaviness of dread.

"She died last night," the colonel tells me.

My throat tightens, and I glance at my hands folded in my lap. Through welling tears, I sense him watching me intently. It feels to me as if he wants to study my reaction to the news of his mama's death.

"Before bed, I always check on her. When I snap on the light, it usually wakes her, but this time she failed to respond. I looked carefully and determined that she was dead."

His voice is flat, and I feel chilled as I glance at him and see an odd movement in his eyes. Beyond the porch screen the river swims in morning light. I feel this beauty protecting me like a shield.

Finally I manage to speak to the colonel. I tell him I knew she'd be my friend from the very first moment I saw her.

"Interesting," he says. He sips from a cup of tea and blots his mouth with a napkin.

"Will there be a service for her here? I'd like to go."

"A prayer will be said at the burial site near what was once the family estate." He bows his head. I feel a stirring of sympathy for him as the colonel reaches into a back pocket, pulls out a handkerchief, and wipes his eyes.

"I am very sorry, Colonel Perkins."

"Yesterday I heard her talking about that imaginary friend of hers, that colored boy, Jonas." His lips twitch. "Even in her last moments it seems Mother preferred imaginings instead of fixing her thoughts on Father and me."

Silence gathers between us until he checks his wristwatch, and I stand. "I'll be going now, sir. If there's anything I can do please tell me."

"Wait a moment." The colonel steps inside the house. He returns carrying his wallet. Standing before me, he opens the wallet to show me the many bills it holds. I give him a questioning look.

He reaches into the wallet and pulls out a wad of cash. "For helping Mother in her final days."

I shake my head and move closer to the door. "I can't take it, sir."

"Really? Why not?"

"It wouldn't be right. Eula Mae's my friend."

"Was," he says. "She's gone now. She'll never come back." He tries to walk with me the rest of the way to the door, but I move ahead of him and step outside.

"You haven't forgotten our little talk about Jonas, I trust? Don't speak of him to anyone." He lightly taps his hand against his thigh.

"I remember what you said, sir." I say this as I turn from him and hurry down the steps.

From behind me he calls, "See that you don't forget it."

I feel his eyes follow me as I cross beneath the pines. I want to shout at him, *She's with her true loves at last. She's with Jonas and Star.* The wind touches my cheek, and I listen as the wind whispers of sorrows ended.

I have nothing more to say to the colonel.

At the edge of the lawn I half slide down the slope to the beach and river below, the gift for Eula Mae in my pocket. I cross the beach and step into the water. The currents are warm around my ankles. They wash me with morning light.

"For you in your new life, Eula Mae. From Gabriella." I reach into my pocket. My fingers close around a heart-shaped stone, and I cast it far away into the river. I know my friend will find it.

The river moves on.

# Chapter 26
# Swim Meet

Kids are lined up to dive in for the swim meet's freestyle competition. I recognize some of them from earlier races. They're all good, but the best swimmer, Trish, is at my side. She's won other events already. Over the summer she's taken on that smooth muscular look of something that spends a whole lot of time in the water—a giant squid, maybe. She smiles at me and moves one shoulder and then the other in a circular motion. She gazes along the length of the pool. "You don't look like you'll make it to the other end," she says.

Hawkins had warned me competitors will often try to rattle their rivals, even when they're friends.

"Worry about yourself, Trish. You know I'll make it." The truth is I'm not sure I'll even make it into the pool. Or if I do, it'll be because I've fainted.

I'm trying to calm myself by deep breathing. But now I worry that with my next breath the swimsuit Trish gave me is going to split at the seams. I test it. Everything holds.

The sun's dipping low in the sky as a shrill whistle blows. When I surface, other kids in the race are churning ahead. Trish is way out in front. My heart sinks. Then I remember Emmett. He was a fighter. I think of Hawkins. He's a fighter, and he'd told me I'm one, too––"a warrior." I better do something to earn his belief in me. I quit feeling sorry for myself and get busy.

Breathe. Reach. I force myself to keep going faster until it feels as though my muscles and bones are smashing through one wall and then another, until it feels like I'm swimming out of my skin. Hawkins and the river and Emmett have made this possible. Over the summer they've changed me.

Lights flash in my head. My lungs burn. Voices call to me from the water that rushes by like a river. It sounds like they're chanting, "Win! Win!" But then I hear the voices more clearly. They're singing, "Swim! Swim!"

Trish is directly ahead now. She must've gotten a cramp or swallowed a sickening amount of chlorine for me to get this close. I pull ahead of her. Less than a second later a powerful stream of water pushes against my side. It's Trish zooming by.

Then it's over. I raise my head, gulping air. Trish is already at the wall.

"Congratulations," I manage between breaths.

Trish turns to me. "You made me swim faster than I thought I'd ever have to." Her face is red from exertion.

The water moves between us, tugging at us. I pull air deep into my lungs before climbing the ladder to the deck to look around for Hawkins. Without Hawkins, I couldn't have entered the race. I want to thank him.

That morning I'd gone into the kitchen to remind him about the swim meet. He was helping a man named Anderson prepare a casserole. Hawkins has been training him.

I told Hawkins I was counting on him being here. The general wouldn't be able to make it because he had an appointment at Bellriver Manor.

"I'll do my best to get away and see you swim, Miss Gabriella." Hawkins had spoken quietly, his eyes catching mine. "I can't promise, though. I'll be over there working at a party in one of the dining rooms."

Anderson leaned with his back against the sink, a dishtowel draped over his shoulder.

"Hawkins is going to be a restaurant king with that place he's opening in Atlanta soon." There was admiration in Anderson's voice.

I had nothing to say to this. I refuse to think about or talk about Hawkins going to Atlanta.

Now I'm searching for him in a sea of white faces around the pool. I look up at the club dining room's large picture window. Several stewards stand at the window looking down. The men are far enough away that I can't be sure Hawkins is with them.

The pool water sloshes against the walls. For a moment I picture Hawkins in the pool. With his long legs and arms he'd swim fast, the aqua water parting for him. I'd never swum with Hawkins. I look away from the pool.

Doyle's near the snack bar. He waves and starts toward me through the crowd. I hurry into the locker room. I don't want to talk to anyone right now. In the locker room I quickly dress. I bundle my suit in with my towel. I'm walking to the general's quarters when Doyle catches up with me.

"Hey, you aren't upset, are you? You swam really well."

"I'm okay."

I guess he senses I'm not. He sticks with me anyway, walking along in silence.

We pass by houses where basketballs and baseball bats clutter driveways and lawns. There's the smell of food cooking and the sound of laughter and dogs barking. Early in the summer the whole world had seemed empty. Maybe there'd been people in those quarters all along. I just hadn't been able to see them for worrying about myself.

In the distance the general's house waits beneath old trees. Its windows are dark. Its shadow is a tattered cape flung across the lawn.

Doyle holds the screen door open as I walk inside. "Will you be here later? I want to play a song for you I just learned."

"I'll always want to hear your songs," I tell him. "I'll be here."

I watch him head to his quarters. Then I walk through the house. I switch on lamps in all its rooms. When Doyle comes over, he'll see the warm lights. It feels like a first step toward making this place a home.

# Chapter 27
# My Future: Name Tags

The general flicks ashes into the little dish beside his plate. We're sitting at the long table in the dining room. "Betty Smith gave me a report on the swim meet. She said you nearly came in first but that her daughter, Trish, won."

"Yes, sir."

I straighten my shoulders and sip from a glass of water. It feels like the right time to explain why he should let me stay at Rock Point. But the general has more to say.

"This time next year you will come in first. I regret that St. Agatha's Boarding School doesn't have a pool. But you will find a way to practice. Swimming is an excellent form of discipline for mind, body and spirit."

I fix my eyes on him. "Sir, I don't believe I should be sent away to school again."

Anderson comes into the room with a platter of meat and potatoes. When he's finished serving, he pushes against the swinging door and steps back into the kitchen. The general stares at me across a bloody slab of beef.

"What did you say?"

Sip water. Set the glass down. "I believe I've earned the right to stay at Rock Point, sir. I just showed I can be pretty good at something on my own. I want to go to school here. That will mean I can help Mama when she comes home. We'll be a family again."

Beyond the window, battleship clouds move over the river. "What makes you think you can help your mother?" The muscle in one side of his jaw snaps.

"Well, sir, when you've been away, lots of times I've..." He doesn't let me finish.

"You need not concern yourself with her situation. Sending you to St. Agatha's is the best choice for everyone. End of subject." Muscles snap in both sides of his jaw.

I push my chair back and stand.

"Mama says her going away was her own idea. She *lies*! You did it. You sent her to Bellriver and me to boarding school because *nothing and no one's good enough for you*. I came in second, but I could barely even swim at the start of the summer until Hawkins showed me." I'm nearly shouting.

The general's out of his chair and coming toward me. He lifts his hand above his shoulder. He's about to strike me across my face. But suddenly a look of agony comes over him. He stumbles back, his hand dropping to his side. He stares at me.

"Don't let me ever again hear you say your mother lies. She told you the truth. She didn't want you seeing her the way she is now."

Our eyes lock.

"As for boarding school..." He walks to a window that looks out across the river. "It's the right solution."

As if from a great distance, I hear him say, "Get started sewing name tags on the sheets, towels, and clothes you'll pack for school if they aren't labeled already. I'm going out now."

He pauses at the door. "I thought you knew how to swim." He pulls the door closed behind him.

I wait until I hear the car door slam and the sound of its motor starting. Then I race to the wide river.

# Chapter 28
# Swept Away

My hands are fists at my sides as I watch the river rushing by. The general's sending me to boarding school. Mama isn't coming home. Hawkins is leaving. I'll go deep in the water where nothing and nobody can touch me. I'll leave everyone behind.

Through a blur of rain I see a shape like a body carried by the hurrying river. My thoughts spin wildly. I know that Emmett's buried in a cemetery in Chicago. Still, I wade in to get a closer look. The currents lift me off my feet. I swim with the currents, and they carry me close to what I want to see.

It's a tree's mid-section. I'm trying to hold onto one of its branches when stars explode in my head, and suddenly the water becomes smooth and clear. It's the color of turquoise. Mermaids with wavy hair swim by. The wind drops. Mist rises from the river. From the mist, a hand reaches toward me. The mist rolls off enough for me to see Emmett Till standing close by.

"A big storm's coming across the river," I tell him.

Emmett laughs. "I'm not afraid."

"Well, I do know that much about you, Emmett Till. Those men tried to force you to say you weren't as good as them. They beat you. But you never would say what they wanted you to say. You're brave and proud. Please, Emmett, teach me."

Slanting bronze-gold light replaces the mist. Emmett's eyes are filled with that same light.

"There's something I want to show you. Come on, Gabriella. Take my hand." Emmett has the handsomest face and smile.

He leads me to a place of blooming flowers and trees filled with fruit. Birds spread rainbow feathers. Animals rest in the sun. In the distance, horses race over green fields.

People crowd around an old man playing a guitar, and children dance to his music. Others gather at a stage to watch a play. Emmett and I stroll through an outdoor market offering vegetables and fruits, spices, cheese, and every kind of bread imaginable. The young help the old, the strong help the weak. All the different races mingle peacefully.

"Is this Atlantis?"

Emmett only smiles.

"Please let me stay with you."

"Gabriella, you are meant to live and love on earth. You need do nothing else."

"My heart doesn't know how to give love. I feel so empty."

Emmett walks a few steps before turning so that we face each other. What he says next I hear only as a whisper. Still, it's every bit a command. "Help others know they aren't alone. That is love, Gabriella. Carry me in your heart, and you'll never be empty."

I stare into Emmett's eyes. But it's Hawkins's eyes like the river that meet mine from his scarred face.

"All right, Miss Gabriella. All right, then. You're going to be just fine," Hawkins is saying.

With my arms around his neck, he carries me from the water onto the beach. Everything's rocking. Everything's swaying.

"I need to sit."

Hawkins bends low and sets me on the sand. I lean forward. The water I swallowed gushes out. Hawkins finds a wet bandana. He uses it to wipe my face.

The storm's heading south now. Nearby the slope no longer sways. I sit up and look around.

"Feeling better, young lady?"

"Uh-huh. I think so. Yes."

Hawkins looks toward the edge of the lawn. "Colonel Perkins is on his way."

I stagger to my feet. The colonel comes closer, and I see that he's gripping a dark object flat against his thigh.

Hawkins steps forward to meet him. "Colonel, what's the gun for? What's this about?"

"I saw everything between you and the girl. You're coming with me, boy." The colonel lifts his arm and points the weapon at Hawkins.

"No, sir."

"You would disobey my order?"

"First, put the weapon away, colonel. Let me explain."

"You dare tell me what to do?" Flecks of spit collect on the colonel's lips. "You ought to be pistol-whipped for impudence."

Hawkins's voice is soothing. Yet he grows more commanding by the minute. "Let Miss Gabriella go home. Then we can talk, sir."

The gun wobbles as the colonel reaches out to grab at my shirt with his free hand.

"She's going with me. I'll protect her from you," the colonel screams.

"No!" For a moment I don't recognize that the harsh cry is my own.

"Colonel, sir, that gun might go off."

"And when it does, I expect you'll die." He waves the gun at Hawkins.

I drop to my knees, scoop up wet sand, and hurl it at the colonel's eyes. He staggers, cursing. At that moment Hawkins kicks the gun from Perkins's hand.

The colonel doubles over with a moan, his hand gripped tight to his chest. Hawkins shoves him aside while I grab the gun. I hand it to Hawkins. He empties it of bullets and thrusts it in his waistband.

"What in the name of hell's going on here?" The muscles in both sides of the general's jaw snap.

Perkins speaks in a furious voice. "I saw it all. That colored boy Hawkins held Gabriella in his arms. She had her arms around his neck. They've been in the river together."

The general turns to Hawkins. "What happened?"

I speak up before Hawkins can say anything.

"Sir, I went into the river. I was drowning."

"No dramatics, Gabriella. Just tell what happened."

"And then Hawkins saved me, sir."

Colonel Perkins stares at Hawkins. Not exactly a movement or a shape but some combination comes to the surface now in the colonel's bulging eyes. And then it's burrowing deep into the colonel's skull. Until the next time.

Above, stars shine, and in the fresh wind wet leaves rustle. The moon is rising. I will walk between the general and Hawkins. They will protect me and each other. But they cannot erase the evil I just saw in the colonel's eyes.

# Chapter 29
# An Empty Room

I'd seen cardboard boxes on Hawkins's doorstep. Still his going any place other than to the river, to his or our quarters, didn't seem real. I'd refused to think about his leaving. But below my bedroom window, Hawkins and the general are talking. Hawkins tells him he's taking the seven o'clock train to Atlanta.

This evening.

"I've come to collect a few last things." The two men shake hands.

"Gabriella was reading in her room a while ago. She'll want to say good-bye."

"Yes, sir."

I struggle against the tightening in my throat. His tour of duty has ended, and he's going to Atlanta. It might as well be Atlantis at the bottom of the sea.

Hawkins and the general are walking toward the stewards' quarters. Hawkins is pointing to its sagging roof, the flakes of paint. The general listens.

Someone's calling my name. I go downstairs and find Trish on the front stoop. She snaps her gum and offers me a stick of Juicy Fruit. We shoot baskets at her quarters. We listen to records in her room.

Trish asks why every couple of minutes I'm looking out the window. "You're hoping to see Doyle?"

I'm hiding from Hawkins. I don't want to see him leave. When I think it's safe to go, Trish sees me to the door. Back home, I immediately look for him. The thing is, I do want to say something to him even though I'm not sure what that is exactly.

He's not at his quarters. The wind cries through dry leaves down by the river. Two dragonflies hover over the water. They dart here and there, and then they are gone. Where they were the air sparkles, like they'd polished it with their wings. This is all they were ever meant to do in this place where they will never be again.

It's cold in the shadowed woods. I'm shivering by the time I reach Hawkins's quarters again and press my face close to the screen door. I call to him. When there's no answer, I open the door and step inside.

The room is dark with the yellow-brown light of an old window shade. Water droplets cover the few dishes left to dry at the sink. A broom is propped in a corner. *He was here moments ago.*

I peer in the empty closet. *He's waiting for me somewhere in here.* I turn away. *If only he'd come through the door.* I sprawl across the mattress, burying my face in its folds.

I'm wheeling my bike from the garage when the general comes around the side of our quarters.

"Where have you been, Gabriella? You missed seeing Hawkins off. He's fixed us some chow. Come on. Let's eat."

I'm tempted to lie about where I'm heading because the general might not let me go. But I know for a fact he respects Hawkins. I think he's beginning to like me, too. The evening of the storm when the general drove off, he turned back because he was worried about me.

"Can we eat later, sir? I want to go to the train station."

I see pain in the general's eyes. I think I know the reason.

"I know you aren't sending Hawkins away. Just like I know you didn't send me or Mama away because you think we aren't good enough. I'm sorry I said those untrue things."

The general removes his uniform hat and holds it in his hands. "We'll go see your mother, Gabriella. We'll go soon."

"Yes, sir."

At the start of summer when he'd picked me up at the airport to drive us to Rock Point, the general had handed me a road map. *You be the navigator*, he'd said. Now I think we're navigating ourselves home at last.

# Chapter 30
# Hawkins's Name

I draw in a ragged breath and let it out. Hawkins is standing beside a wall on the far side of the waiting room. He doesn't know I'm here. I march over and stand close to him.

When Trish and I spied on him he knew we were in the bushes. He scowled at us then. But now when he looks down at me, I get to see that scar of his wrinkle with his surprised smile.

"Miss Gabriella, I didn't think I'd see you again."

"When you open your restaurant, I'll be there." I can already see myself sitting at a table with Hawkins. We are drinking Cokes in frosted glasses and eating hamburgers.

But now we're in the "Coloreds" section of the train station. There isn't a single fan in here and no place to sit. Hawkins pulls a bandana from his pocket and wipes the moisture from his face.

"Let's step outside," he says.

I have many questions for him. I dive right into the middle of them.

"Did you teach me to swim because you had to?" *He'll say yes, he taught me to swim because I'm the general's daughter.*

"Yes, ma'am, I certainly did."

He sees my disappointment.

"Miss Gabriella, I didn't want you drowning. That was why I *had* to teach you to swim. There was another reason, too."

"What else?" *Now he'll tell the truth.*

"Something bigger than you or me decided from the moment we met that we should become friends."

"Forever?"

He nods. "Forever." Then he gives me a long look. "Though you swore to me you never would, Miss Gabriella, you went in the water by yourself." His scowl is terrifying.

I'd let Hawkins down.

"It won't happen again, sir."

"All right, young lady, just see that it doesn't."

The train gives a sudden screeching jolt. Hawkins picks up his suitcase. I'm wrestling with what I want to say before he goes.

"I only know you as Hawkins."

We're walking along the platform. He smiles across his big shoulder at me. "Calling me Hawkins is just fine. But so you'll have the satisfaction of knowing my first name, it's Robert. Robert Apollo Hawkins."

"Apollo. For the sun?"

"Yes, ma'am. There's a theater in New York's Harlem with that name, too. My parents met there."

We come to a stop. Instead of climbing on board, Hawkins sets his suitcase down, unfastens its lid, and reaches inside. Passengers flow around us like we're boulders in a stream. What he's looking for is right on top. He closes and refastens the suitcase lid. In his hand he holds a military camouflage cap, the kind worn every day by Marines.

"This is for you." He fits the cap on my head.

"Thank you, Robert Hawkins."

"You are welcome, Gabriella Winter."

He makes a small adjustment to the cap. Then he stands back to examine his work.

"All right." He looks into my eyes. "All right, then."

The train lurches forward. He picks up his suitcase and swings it onto a small metal platform. Below it is a metal stair. He steps onto the stair.

What I want to say is in my heart, not in my head. Maybe that's why I'm not sure how to say it. I'd better do it soon, though. The train begins to slide away from the station.

I walk fast. Hawkins is still standing on the metal stair. I've about given up on myself when what I want to say comes at me like blue lightning from the clear sky. Should I risk saying it? There's nobody around. *Emmett gave me my orders. I am to love.*

The train picks up speed.

"I love you!" The words are lost in the rolling thunder of the train. Still, Hawkins's scarred face seems to ripple like water when wind and light move across it. *He knows.*

He lifts his long arm, as if he's about to swim to me. He lifts his arm high into the red-gold light. Too soon his tall figure grows frail with distance. The train disappears. A mournful cry hollows the air.

I stand with my arms hanging at my sides. The wind moves through the trees. Their limbs sweep shadows over the tracks. Blackbirds flying above the station dip their wings in the lavender light. In the station, my steps echo between crumbling walls.

From somewhere near the voice of a child and the answering voice of a man drift to me before fading away. I step through the station doorway onto hard ground. Far off in the west, the sun drops behind the horizon like an orange slipping from a child's hand.

❧

I'm sitting on the back porch writing a letter to my teacher at boarding school:

"How are you? I hope you are well. I wonder if you remember me, your student Gabriella Winter? I wish you could see how the leaves are beginning to show some red and yellow now. But to tell you the truth, in my heart it's still summer in North Carolina, and I have just seen Hawkins for the first time. We are down by the river."

I tell her Hawkins taught me to swim and saved my life, that weeks have gone by since Hawkins took the train to Atlanta, but that I know I'll see him again. I just know it. Hawkins, I tell her, is the man Emmett would have grown up to be if his life hadn't been so cruelly taken from him.

I hope she'll understand my telling her Emmett's laughter came to me one afternoon when I saw children playing in the river. Emmett was there keeping watch over them just like Hawkins kept watch over me. I write my teacher that for as long as I live, Emmett will live safe in my heart. If I could, I would give him more.

Whenever I look up from my letter writing, I see the lights where Mama is staying across the river. The river took me to her. It will bring her back to me. It's brought me everything this summer.

By the time I finish writing it, the letter is three pages on ruled paper. I fold it and place it in an envelope. I put my teacher's name on the front. The general will have an exact address for the school. He'll like it that I'm staying in touch with my teacher even though I ride the bus to a school outside Rock Point with Doyle and Trish.

Each night after doing my homework, I walk beneath the pines to the edge of the lawn. Tonight a full moon floods the woods. The stars sparkle. My feet sink in the loose soil of the steep slope as I make my way to the river.

I'm running along its shore. I lift my arms and feel the night around me. In the sound of wind and water, Hawkins comes to me. I stop running and kneel by the water, cupping it in my hands. My heart is big. All my loves are with me now. I won't ever leave them behind. There has been rain, and the river shines as it rolls home to the sea.

The End

# To the Reader

Emmett Till was born on July 25, 1941, and had barely turned fourteen when he was beaten and shot, his lifeless body pushed into the Tallahatchie River in Mississippi. Racial hatred ended his young life in the early morning of August 28, 1955. The details of his murder come from the historical record, in particular the January 24, 1956 article by William Bradford Huie published in *Look Magazine.* Over the years books, articles, documentaries, songs, and poems have been created about the Chicago youth who died so brutally. In this work of fiction, Emmett Till is the only figure to have actually lived outside the author's imagination. Today Emmett Till's death is recognized as having helped bring to life the Civil Rights movement. That movement continues to influence us all. In this powerful and enduring way, Emmett Louis Till's spirit lives on.